A BERRY MERRY CHRISTMAS

DEBORAH COOKE

CLAIRE CROSS

DEBORAH A. COOKE

A Berry Merry Christmas
By Deborah Cooke

This novella was originally published under the pseudonym Claire Cross.

 Created with Vellum

PROLOGUE

Toronto—December

DREW SINCLAIR SAT in the vinyl upholstered chair and watched the tiny figure in the hospital bed. Swathed from head to toe, she was unrecognizable as his niece Natalie and for the umpteenth time, Drew hoped she didn't remember anything about how she had gotten here.

Then he hoped, one more time, that the scars from her burns wouldn't leave her marked for life. The last thing he wanted was Natalie thinking of what—or who —she had lost every single time she looked in the mirror.

Who could have guessed that the mice in his brother's rambling country house would chew through the electrical cable that strung the Christmas tree lights together? Drew would have checked them—it was in his nature to double-check everything—so seriously that his brother Greg would have teased him about it.

But Greg would never tease Drew about anything again. A whole week and Drew still couldn't get used to the idea of his happy-go-lucky younger brother being gone.

Forever.

Drew watched Natalie's little chest rise and fall, knowing without a doubt why Greg and Winona had never bothered to trap the attic mice. Natalie thought they were cute and everyone falsely assumed that anything cute must be harmless.

Drew guessed that it had been Natalie who wanted the Christmas lights left on all night and that her parents had seen no harm in indulging her.

He had awakened to his phone ringing in the wee hours of the morning. In no time at all, he was driving north through the snow to the hospital nearest the old farmhouse Greg had been renovating.

"Old wiring" was the conclusion of the fire inspector. Not up to code. And the mice had been busily chewing on more than the string of Christmas lights. The older man had shaken his head while giving Drew the news this very morning and Drew had seen that it wasn't the first time this fire inspector had delivered this kind of news at this time of year. And not only did the older man know it wouldn't be the last—he knew there was precious little he could do about it.

Any way you sliced it, it was one hell of a Christmas present.

Drew gave thanks that he could afford the very best. If he had anything to say about it, Natalie wouldn't have a single physical scar.

Her heart, now, was something he wasn't sure he'd be able to fix.

But he would bloody well try.

The monitor beeped quietly, all the red lights doing what they were supposed to do. The silence of the night permeated the hospital ward and darkness pressed against the window. Drew leaned his elbows on his knees, templed his fingers together and watched for some tiny sign that Natalie was still in there.

"Mr. Sinclair! You're *still* here." The nurse who was always on evenings hovered in the doorway. "Have you gone home at all?"

Drew barely glanced her way. "I need to be here."

The nurse bustled into the room and gave him a stern glance. "Have you eaten?"

"Enough," Drew lied. The truth was he wasn't the least bit interested in food.

"Mr. Sinclair, it's been seven days. This could go on for a long time. You have to take care of yourself—after all, Natalie has no one else left."

A pang shot through Drew's heart at the reminder he didn't really need. "I know," he said softly, his gaze still snared by the bandaged figure on the bed. Natalie looked so much smaller than he knew her to be.

It was the unnatural stillness of her, he guessed. Who ever knew a four-year-old who stopped moving for a moment? And Natalie had been the busiest—and the happiest—of them all.

Would Drew ever see her smile again?

"She needs me here," he said when the nurse seemed to be waiting for him to say something. And the funny thing was that as soon as Drew said the words, he knew them to be true.

That gave him an idea. The nurse made another comment or two, but when Drew didn't answer, she scurried from the room, scanning her clipboard as she went. As soon as the echo of her heels on the linoleum faded, Drew pulled his chair closer to the bed. His heart was racing and he didn't know if he was about to do the dumbest thing he'd ever thought of, but it had to be worth a try.

He was not, after all, an impulsive or whimsical man.

But, despite that, Drew reached down and removed a teddy bear from the bag the fire inspector had brought. Even though it didn't look its best, Drew knew it was a teddy bear, because this was none other than Mr. Bumbles.

Mr. Bumbles had been in pretty rough shape before the fire, having been loved and squeezed by a certain little girl until he was a mere shadow of his former self. Winona had patched him up more than once. He was missing an eye and several much-adored patches of fur were completely worn away.

Now the bear had a few scorch marks to add to his battle wounds, but he was still unmistakably Mr. Bumbles. The fire inspector had evidently heard about Natalie's condition and guessed the ownership of Mr. Bumbles in his search of the site. Mr. Bumbles had a couple of jazzy new bandages and a little sling. The charred fur had been mostly trimmed away.

The fire inspector hadn't said anything at all when he gave the bear to Drew, but Drew had been touched by the compassionate gesture. Complete strangers did the damndest things this time of year. Neither man had said anything about the transaction. One steady look had confirmed both their thoughts, then Drew had placed the bag out of sight.

Now, he gently lifted a small bandaged arm and tucked Mr. Bumbles in the nook of the elbow where he rightly belonged.

Drew waited with bated breath, but nothing happened at all. Unable to account for his sense of failure, he settled back into his chair and pressed his fingertips together once again.

And Natalie moved.

Drew's eyes widened in shock. He blinked, he looked again. Natalie's grip on the bear changed ever so slightly. Her bandaged face turned as though she would brush the tip of her nose across Mr. Bumbles. Her little fingers clenched around the bear's paw and she snuggled him close.

Drew knew he didn't imagine her little sigh of satisfaction. One of the monitors, after all, had picked up its pace. His heart danced around his chest like a wild thing and he couldn't help but grin idiotically.

Natalie was going to be all right.

A WEEK LATER, on the day of Christmas Eve, the doctors took off another round of Natalie's bandages.

It was a challenge, given her death grip on Mr. Bumbles.

Drew was a bit startled to see his niece with her blonde corkscrew curls gone, even though he knew that some had burned in the fire and the rest had been shaved away to treat her burns. One cheek and temple was still an angry red, but the plastic surgeon was confident that it could be set to rights.

She was still a pretty child, with her heart-shaped face and Greg's dimple right in the middle of her chin. Natalie had Winona's blue eyes, although their luxuriant lashes had to grow back. Drew remembered all too well how merrily those eyes danced when Natalie had made some mischief.

He hoped desperately that, one day, she would laugh again.

It took Natalie a few minutes to get used to even the dimmed light in the room, then her serious gaze zeroed in on Drew. The doctor stepped back into the shadows and shooed the nurse away, leaving the two with a comparatively private moment.

Drew's mouth went dry and all the words he'd composed to explain the truth to Natalie completely fled his mind. He stared back at her, feeling more helpless than he ever had in his life.

"Unca Drew?" Her voice was so much more fragile than Drew remembered, but at least she recognized him. The psychologist had been uncertain how heavily traumatized Natalie would be.

How much did she remember of that awful night? All Drew wanted to do was scoop up his niece and protect her from everything nasty in the world, but he was terrified of frightening her. After all, he was just an uncle who visited half a dozen times a year.

Drew forced a little smile. "Yeah, punkin." He had always called her that and he hoped the familiarity would reassure her in this very unfamiliar place. "I'm here."

"You were here before," she said with eerie certainty. "You gave me Mr. Bumbles."

Drew caught his breath. "Yes. I did. He wanted to help you get better."

Natalie hugged the bear closer, licked her chapped lip and scanned the room. She solemnly eyed the doctor before looking to Drew once more.

"Mummy and daddy aren't coming, are they?" she whispered.

Drew tried very hard to swallow the lump in his

throat and failed. He wasn't sure he could summon a word, so he simply shook his head.

Natalie's brow furrowed and she watched the doctor for a moment that stretched long. Her thumb stroked Mr. Bumbles' paw with an intensity fit to wear off what little fur remained on it.

"Not tomorrow neither," she finally said, a soft ring of conviction in her voice. Her clear gaze swiveled to lock with Drew's once more, as though this tiny child would will him to tell her the truth.

It seemed that Natalie remembered quite a lot.

Drew inched his chair closer, never breaking her gaze, then reached out to gently touch her hand. "No. Not tomorrow either, punkin," he confirmed quietly.

Natalie's bottom lip trembled ever so slightly, then a tear cascaded over her cheek. Her mouth worked for a moment, her vulnerability tearing Drew's guts. It wasn't fair that a small child should have to come to terms with such a loss.

Just when Drew thought he could stand it no longer, Natalie took a deep breath and impaled him with a piercing glance. "Are you going to be my daddy now?" she demanded hoarsely.

Drew's heart clenched. He immediately captured Natalie's tiny hand, liking how her fingers curled reflexively around his. He looked into her too-serious eyes, willing her to understand how hard he was going to try to make everything right in her world.

His voice was surprisingly husky, even to his own ears. "You can count on it, punkin."

ONE

Two years later

DEAR SANTA;
CAN YOU BRING ME A NEW MOMMY?
I HAVE BEEN VERY, VERY, <u>VERY</u> GOOD.
MR. BUMBLES SAYS SO.
XoXoX
NATALIE

HOLLY READ THE NOTE TWICE, trying desperately to figure out what this had to do with her. Being called into Mr. C.'s office wasn't usually a good moment for her and she *had* mucked up the paint on those new toy dump trucks this morning.

It wasn't as though she tried to do things wrong—just the opposite, in fact!—but Holly simply wasn't mechanically minded at all. The elves in charge of the North Pole workshop kept inventing clever new devices, almost as though they meant to spite her. It seemed to Holly that those gadgets took one look at her and went wild.

The last time she had stood in this very same place

—after the tragic doll-with-three-eyes incident—Mr. C. had told she would have one more chance. There was no doubt that Holly had blown that chance today. Her mouth went dry. What was going to happen now?

She wasn't sure she wanted to know.

Holly peeked over the note to meet the very serious gaze of Mr. C. himself. She tried to swallow the lump of dread in her throat, but failed. Mrs. C. was even there—less of a good sign to Holly's mind—and both of their expressions were unusually grim.

Holly waved the note. "I, um, I don't understand."

Mr. C. inhaled sharply and strained his red suspenders. "Holly, there's no two ways about it. You just aren't working out among the elves on the floor."

He frowned and pushed his spectacles further up his red-as-a-cherry nose. Holly had never seen him so solemn—even when she had entangled the strings of four hundred and twelve brand new marionettes.

Three weeks ago.

"We can't have elves who don't contribute to the bottom line," he continued, "especially at this time of year when we're heading into very heavy production."

"It's bad for morale, dear," Mrs. C. interjected. "And we can't have *that* when everyone has so much work to do."

"Please, Holly, we're asking you not to go back on the production floor," Mr. C. said.

"Ever," Mrs. C. clarified.

"Under any terms."

Holly's heart sank like a stone. That could mean only one thing.

She was being fired.

From the North Pole workshop. Holly was quite certain that elves didn't get work anywhere else.

"Now, don't look so crestfallen, dear. We know that it isn't really your fault," Mrs. C. continued quickly, her hands wringing in her apron. "We know you have a heart of gold, Holly, and perhaps you just haven't found your *niche*." She licked her lips and frowned in turn. "There's just something about you that makes everything run amuck. You have some kind of...*gift*, dear."

It didn't feel like much of a gift to Holly.

"Damndest thing." Mr. C. scowled. "And very inconvenient."

Mrs. C. summoned a pert smile. "So, dear, you'll just have to stay out of the workshop for good."

Holly finally found her voice. "But what will I do?"

"Well!" Mrs. C.'s expression brightened considerably. "We've found just the thing for you, dear. Tell her, Nowell."

"Very tricky job," Mr. C. said gruffly. "But you just might have the necessary talent to get it done."

Holly wondered whether they needed something broken somewhere.

Mr. C. took off his glasses and fixed Holly with his blue gaze, pointing his glasses at the note she held. "Charming little girl, this Natalie. Orphaned two years back, adopted by her bachelor uncle. As you can see, she wants a new mommy."

Mr. C. cleared his throat when Holly said nothing. "I suspect he's afraid to continue on with his life, now that the niece is his responsibility. Drew Sinclair seems to be the kind to take responsibility very seriously. Could stand to lighten up, actually, although that isn't exactly what we want you to do."

Holly knew she looked blank.

Mrs. C. leaned forward, her eyes sparkling. "You

see, dear, we're quite certain there's just a little mix-up here. Tell her, Nowell."

Mr. C. put his glasses back on and scanned a fax on his desk. "Well, there's a certain Katherine O'Neill who has some idea about marrying this uncle." Mr. C. flicked Holly a stern glance. "I discovered this through quite unorthodox channels, by the way, and I'd like to keep the whole thing very hush-hush."

"Of course, sir."

Mr. C. nodded. "The way I see it, the bottleneck here is Mr. Drew Sinclair. What we want you to do is go on down there to Toronto and set things in motion." He checked his watch. "It's the seventeenth of December and Christmas is an awfully nice time to propose marriage, after all. Wouldn't you say, Noel?"

"Oh, Nowell!" Mrs. C. blushed like a schoolgirl. "Holly doesn't want to know all about *that!*"

A merry twinkle took up residence in Mr. C.'s eyes. "What do you say, Holly? This could be the beginning of a bright future for you."

"I can't imagine how *anything* could go wrong!" Mrs. C. trilled with obvious excitement. "It's so perfectly simple!"

Holly, though, had her doubts. "Won't they notice that I'm an elf? I mean, the ears do give it away." She fingered the telltale points on her ears, then held up one foot. The bell on one toe jingled. "Not to mention the shoes."

"We can conceal the ears, dear, and I've had a mortal wardrobe prepared for you."

Mr. C. shuffled through the paperwork on his desk. "And we've worked out a cover for you. Oddly enough —" he winked "—Natalie's nanny quit very suddenly this morning. Mr. Sinclair is in a bit of a fix, since he does have a day job where a six-year-old child would get in the way. He's interviewing nannies at this very moment—we've prepared an excellent résumé for you, complete with impeccable references."

He looked Holly dead in the eye. "You'll get the nanny job, that much I can ensure."

"But the rest, dear," Mrs. C. added softly, "is entirely up to you."

As she looked back at them, Holly knew that she held what was her very last chance in the grip of her hand. She had to make this work or she would be a very unemployed, yet still immortal elf.

It would be tough to scrape by for all eternity.

Holly *had* to succeed.

She swallowed and nodded with false confidence. "I'll do it. When do I start?"

The pair before her smiled with satisfaction. "Right now," Mr. C. confirmed.

Before Holly could ask, he lifted his hand, palm flat. She saw the glitter of fairy dust for just an instant before Mr. C. pursed his lips and blew.

Then Holly was surrounded by dancing crystals, not unlike swirling snowflakes. A warm wind picked her up and tumbled her along with them as though she weighed no more than a snowflake herself. She rolled helplessly, surrounded by dancing silver and light, and wished with all her heart she would succeed.

HOLLY LANDED square on her feet on the sidewalk in front of a brick house. It was not unlike the houses on either side of it. The well-tended lawn and garden were deadened and waiting for spring, the cedars bound in burlap, although there was no snow just yet.

Holly looked down to find her clothes completely changed. She was wearing a dark green jacket that was nice and warm. A peppermint striped scarf was wound around her neck. Her slim-fitting trousers were a deep shade of red and she peeked to find herself wearing a lovely creamy sweater that was embroidered with prancing reindeer. She had a large black purse slung over her shoulder and neat black boots upon her feet, a small black suitcase rested beside her on the sidewalk.

The combination would go well with her dark hair and green eyes. And goodness knew, Holly wanted to look her very best for such an important job. The little black boots didn't even have pointed toes.

A glitter caught her eye, and she discovered a merry Santa brooch pinned to her jacket. Just the sight of it made Holly smile. She reached up and found the peaks gone from her ears, much to her relief. And little earrings, although she couldn't tell what shape they were. They jingled when Holly moved her head.

All in all, Mrs. C. had done quite well. Holly glanced up and down the street and imagined she looked perfectly mortal. A thrill of anticipation rolled through her.

Maybe she really *could* do this job!

She looked back to the house, not quite sure how to proceed. Was this the right place? Bay windows flanked the front door, and she noticed that this house —unlike its neighbors—had absolutely no Christmas decorations at all.

How odd.

Maybe they just hadn't gotten around to decorating yet. After all, Mr. C. had said that this uncle had his plate full with the nanny leaving so suddenly. The front door was a cheerful bright red, though, and with her keen elvish vision, Holly could see the name engraved on the brass door knocker.

Sinclair.

This must be the place. She took a deep breath and hoped desperately that she wouldn't screw this up. That resolved, Holly marched right up the path and rang the bell.

The door cracked open just an instant later, although it moved slowly, as though someone was having difficulty pulling it wide. When the crack widened to about a foot, a head poked around in the vicinity of the doorknob.

It was a little girl, her hair short around her head. The light from the house got caught in the fair curls and made her look like she wore a halo.

What a darling child! Holly would have cast her as a cherub in the angelic host without a second thought.

This must be Natalie.

Holly smiled, quite genuinely pleased to meet the girl who had written to Mr. C. It took some gumption to ask for what you really wanted, after all.

But Natalie's eyes went round as she scanned Holly from head to toe. "You're Christmas!" she exclaimed.

Holly laughed. "No. Just Holly. Holly Berry."

Before Natalie could say anything else, the door was quickly opened from behind. Holly's gaze rode up, way up, until she met the steely grey eyes of the very tall man standing right behind Natalie. His shoulders were broad, his navy pinstripe suit trim, his burgundy tie crisply knotted. The white hanky peeked out of his pocket at the perfect angle.

His hair was a chestnut brown, his temples touched with just the right measure of silver to make him look distinguished. In fact, he might have been a handsome man, if he hadn't looked so grim, because his jaw was square and his nose aquiline.

Holly had a funny feeling that the exactitude of his profile suited him perfectly. His eyes were so relentless in their appraisal that Holly felt herself flush a little bit. She was pretty sure she hadn't measured up to his first survey of her assets.

She knew without a shadow of a doubt who he was. Because if ever there had been a man who needed to "lighten up," he had to be the one standing right in front of her.

This was Drew Sinclair.

Even though he was much younger than she had anticipated. Holly guessed that he was somewhere in his early thirties, mortally speaking, and took another look. Here she had been expecting a sweet and kindly older man who would take readily to her suggestion that he pop the question to the equally sweet and kindly older Katherine O'Neill.

But Holly couldn't even begin to imagine how she would make this man do anything he hadn't already decided to do.

It seemed she *could* screw up this job, after all.

And that conclusion made Holly's heart sink straight to her toes.

DREW SINCLAIR WAS FED UP.

A dozen nanny interviews already this morning

and not a single applicant with sufficient sense that he would entrust Natalie to her care. In fact, he wasn't sure the women he had met could be trusted to find their own way back home without incident.

He'd kept Natalie home from school to see her response to each applicant, but he was starting to feel as though the entire morning had been an exercise in futility. Drew wasn't being overly protective, he knew it.

He was just being *sensible*.

It could have been his middle name, after all.

Natalie's greeting of this candidate had brought Drew's protective instincts screaming to the fore. Christmas! The last thing they needed was any reminder that it was Christmas—and an anniversary of the worst kind. Drew was prepared to dislike this Holly Berry on sight when he pulled open the door.

But he didn't.

In fact, Drew found her very attractive.

That was so remarkable, so ridiculous, so utterly illogical that it made him frown. Drew had long ago abandoned his quest to find a suitable life partner—it was a bit startling to find the most intriguing woman he'd seen in years standing right on his doorstep.

He didn't know quite what to do.

So, he had a better look, certain that nonsensical attraction would just disappear upon further inspection.

But Holly Berry was tall and trim, apparently with curves in all the right places. Her dark hair was neatly cropped at her chin and its waves bounced with a life of their own. She wore no makeup, at least none that Drew could discern, and he noted with approval that her prettiness needed no such accent. Her full ruddy lips curved as though she was on the verge of laughter.

It was her eyes, though, that snared Drew's attention. They were thickly lashed and tipped up at the outer corners with delightful femininity. That would be interesting enough, but their color was incredible. Ms. Berry's eyes were the most unusual shade of silver grey, and they sparkled as though they were filled with stardust.

That was by far the most fanciful thought Drew had ever permitted to set foot in his orderly mind, but it was exactly right. He stared and he marveled and he knew that he would never see another pair of eyes so beautiful.

That was absurd. Drew frowned a little more severely, just for good measure.

Amazingly, Ms. Berry didn't seem to pick up on Drew's sour mood at all. Her smile was unfailingly sunny. The longer he looked at her, the better Drew felt, although he knew that was crazy.

He had the weirdest urge to smile right back.

"Hello, I'm Holly Berry," she repeated. Her voice was low and curiously pleasing. That promise of laughter clung to her words in a most intriguing way. "And you must be Mr. Drew Sinclair."

Drew tried to look stern. "Yes. I am."

Ms. Berry held his gaze for an intoxicatingly long moment, then those full lips quirked. "Might I come in?" she asked mildly, then glanced at Natalie and back at Drew before arching a dark brow. "We wouldn't want anyone to catch cold."

Belatedly, Drew realized they were still standing on the front step. Good thing someone was thinking! What had happened to *his* solid good sense?

Not to mention his manners?

Drew shook his head as though to clear his

thoughts of nonsense, then stepped back and gestured to the foyer behind him. "Won't you come in? Perhaps I could see your résumé?"

She stepped over the threshold, that smile faltering momentarily when Drew extended his hand. Ms. Berry frowned, then grasped at her purse as though it was a lifesaver. "It *must* be in here," she declared cheerfully, then rummaged in the bag with purpose.

Drew blinked. How could she not even know whether or not she had a résumé with her?

That couldn't be a good sign. Not at all. Maybe she really wasn't any different from all the other candidates. Drew glanced to his niece to find her avidly eying the woman on the doorstep.

Now, *that* was something. Natalie hadn't been nearly so interested in anyone else. Drew looked back to the potential nanny and deliberately gave her the benefit of the doubt.

Anyone could have a moment's disorganization. Couldn't they?

Drew wasn't entirely sure, not being able to recall having had one himself.

Ms. Berry gave a cry of delight and victoriously produced a creamy envelope from the depths of her bag. She smiled with her previous confidence and presented it to Drew with a flourish.

Her hands, he noticed immediately, were slender and long-fingered. Her nails were carefully trimmed and buffed, her fingers were ring-free. And Drew liked those hands very much, though he didn't dare to examine precisely which element prompted his approval.

But, Drew *never* noticed people's hands. Obviously, the inconvenience of this morning was getting to him. He accepted the envelope quickly, minimizing the moment their fingers brushed.

All the same, his hand tingled slightly from the brief contact with fingertips. Drew felt as though he had lost an opportunity for...something.

He'd definitely been working too hard.

He gave the envelope his most forbidding survey to get his mind back on track. Drew's name was neatly typed on the front, his address below. The stationary was a nice choice, a good quality stock but not too expensive. Drew was impressed.

Even though there was still one thing bothering him. "How could you not know that you had this with you?"

Ms. Berry laughed, a sound that made Drew think of hundreds of silver bells pealing simultaneously. Or a sparkling mountain waterfall. "I'm sorry but it's been a very odd morning," she said and smiled right into his eyes.

The foyer suddenly seemed a little bit warm to Drew.

Oddly reassured and wanting to reassure her in turn, Drew let his lips curve just a little bit. "It's been a bit hectic here this morning, as well, Ms. Berry," he acknowledged.

"*Ms. Berry!*" she echoed and wrinkled her nose in a charming way. "Everyone just calls me Holly, Mr. Sinclair. You have to do the same, I insist."

Drew found himself clearing his throat. He had called other nannies by their first names—why did Holly's suggestion seem so...intimate?

"I'm not certain that would be appropriate, Ms. Berry," he began in his best banker voice, but his niece wasn't going to let him finish.

"I'll call you Holly," Natalie interjected from the region of Drew's knees. Drew glanced down in surprise. She didn't usually take that quickly to strangers.

But then, Holly was so engaging that she didn't seem like a stranger.

"Good!" Holly declared before Drew could wrap his mind around the fact that he was already thinking of this woman in such friendly terms. "You must be Natalie," Holly said and turned her smile on Drew's niece.

Drew's heartstrings tugged when Natalie nodded shyly. "I am." The little girl's brow puckered for a moment.

"What is it?" Holly prompted with concern before Drew could ask. Natalie bit her lip and Holly leaned closer, raising one fingertip to her lips. "You can whisper it to me," she confided, "if you need to."

Natalie flicked a glance at her uncle, then stepped toward Holly to do exactly that. Drew's chest clenched.

"Do those bells ring?" Natalie pointed to Holly's earrings.

Holly smiled. "Let's find out." She deliberately shook her head. The move filled the foyer with a sparkling sound of tiny ringing bells. Natalie gasped with delight.

Then, Holly laughed again as she tugged the earrings from her ears. "Here. You can have them."

"Can I? Really?" Natalie's eyes were round with wonder.

"Of course!" Holly fitted the clip-on's to an enraptured Natalie's tiny ears with quick fingers.

But Drew couldn't let her do this. "Ms. Berry, you're very generous, but..."

"But, nothing," Holly interrupted Drew flatly. "Natalie likes them and I want her to have them." She closed the clasp on the second earring and sat back on her heels. Natalie shook her head tentatively, her eyes shining when that sound filled the foyer once more. Her lips parted and Drew held his breath.

But Natalie bit back what might have become a smile. Drew's heart sank as his niece danced away, shaking her head to make the bells ring even more.

It was a lovely gesture, but he couldn't let Natalie accept the gift. It was inappropriate.

Drew lowered his voice so that his niece wouldn't hear his protest. "But, Ms. Berry, I really must insist…"

Holly straightened, brushed off her trim burgundy trousers, and met Drew's gaze steadily. She was nearly as tall as him and she smelled faintly of peppermint.

Drew's heart chose this very illogical moment to skip a beat and his words, quite uncharacteristically, faltered mid-argument.

"Mr. Sinclair," she said firmly, her voice pitched low. "This has nothing to do with whether or not you choose to hire me." She looked into his eyes and Drew saw sincerity shining there. "Natalie can have the earrings either way."

"But"—Drew frowned—"you don't need to do this."

"Of course I don't!" Holly's lips twisted into a beguiling smile. She leaned closer to tap a fingertip on his perfectly knotted tie and Drew caught his breath. "Haven't you heard, Mr. Sinclair? It's *Christmas*, a season of giving, a season for making little girls and boys smile."

Could Holly really make Natalie smile again? It had been so long, Drew was halfway certain his niece never would smile, much less laugh again.

But she had already taken to Holly in a big way.

Natalie came running down the hall in that moment, the tinkling of the bells right with her. "Can I keep them, Unca Drew? Can I?"

The last of Drew's resistance to the gift disappeared when he noticed the shine in Natalie's eyes. "That's what Ms. Berry says," he conceded gruffly. "Now, remember your manners."

Natalie turned to Holly and folded her hands before herself. "Thank you very much, Holly, for the jingle bell earrings," she said, then reached out and impulsively touched Holly's hand. Her gaze met Drew's and then flicked away, her words fell in a breathless rush. "I hope you stay *forever!*"

As though embarrassed by this confession, Natalie fled into the kitchen. Drew blinked and watched her go.

It seemed that Holly already had one vote in her favor.

Holly smiled. "She's absolutely adorable," she murmured and turned that smile on Drew as though giving him the credit.

It made absolutely no sense, but Drew felt warm right to his toes. He wasn't impulsive, of course, but there was something about Holly—and Natalie's response to her—that made Drew suspect that she might be the perfect candidate for this job. Naturally, he'd have to take a few moments to check Holly's references before making his decision.

But a part of Drew knew the decision *was* made. He ushered Holly into his office and fiercely hoped that there were no surprises in the envelope he held.

Oddly enough, his printer began to beep an error message as soon as Holly stepped into the room. Drew was sure it couldn't be out of toner and he wasn't printing anything. He apologized as he crossed the room to reset the machine.

He arrived just in time to catch the blank sheet of paper the machine spewed onto the floor. To Drew's astonishment, that was just the beginning of a barrage of sheets that came in rapid-fire succession. He snatched them out of the air, pushed the Reset button, but the machine beeped merrily. It kept flinging paper at him with what seemed to be joyful abandon.

Drew pushed Reset again and again, but to no avail. Paper cascaded from his grip and he wondered what sort of an idiot Holly must think he was. He felt his ears heat and bit back a curse as the machine blithely ignored his efforts to silence it. Finally, Drew bent and hauled the plug from the wall.

To his relief, the machine subsided with one last defiant beep.

He turned to Holly, only to find that she looked more startled than he was. When their gazes met, Drew indulged his urge to smile at her.

He did so only to reassure her that this sort of thing didn't happen all the time, of course. The last thing he wanted was for her to decline this job.

In fact, Drew felt a sudden urgency to hire her as soon as possible. It must be because Natalie liked her so much. Or because he had already moved his nine-thirty appointment twice and couldn't possibly do it again.

It had nothing to do with the fact that Holly Berry had the most intriguing eyes of any woman Drew had ever met.

"I'm sorry about the interruption," he said with all the charm he could muster. Drew knew he didn't look quite as credible as he liked, what with the clutch of loose paper in his hands. "I don't know what went wrong."

To Drew's disappointment, Holly didn't smile back. She bit her lip and took the seat Drew indicated, her glance flicking to the subdued printer.

Almost guiltily.

But that made no sense at all.

Maybe she was just nervous.

Well, he could do something about that. Drew decisively chucked the paper in the recycling bin and set to putting formalities out of the way.

TWO

AN HOUR LATER, Holly was still shaken by her response to Drew Sinclair's smile. It was just because she had never seen a mortal man smile, she told herself as Natalie waved goodbye to her uncle from the living room window.

It was just because Holly hadn't expected this man to *ever* smile. It must have been surprise that made her heart go thumpity-thump in her ears.

It wouldn't happen again, Holly just knew it. She was here to do a job and she was going to do it right. All the same, the house felt oddly empty once Drew's car disappeared around the corner.

Natalie didn't seem to share Holly's view. She took Holly's hand and tugged her toward the stairs. "Come on! I'll show you your room."

Holly scooped up her bag on the way through the foyer and followed the little girl to the third floor of the house. Natalie ran ahead on the last flight of stairs and disappeared through the only doorway at the summit. Holly followed and caught her breath on the threshold.

One big room filled the space beneath the eaves and winter sunlight slanted through the skylights. The ceiling was sloped, all of it wallpapered in a yellow and blue floral print. The furniture was bleached pine, the mood welcoming.

"This is for me?"

"And you have a bathroom, too." Natalie indicated the ensuite bath, then bounced on the bed. Holly unpacked her things and tried to look as though this was perfectly normal for her, even though she didn't know what was in her bag. It was hard to keep from gasping with delight as she unfolded each garment Mrs. C. had provided.

"I'm hungry," Natalie declared abruptly.

Holly vaguely recalled something about mortals *needing* to eat. Elves merely snacked when the mood struck them and often went months—particularly during the demanding pre-holiday season—without eating anything at all.

Holly wondered what mortals ate.

And how often.

She tried to sound nonchalant. "What would you like to eat?"

Natalie didn't even need to consider this. "A peanut butter sandwich."

Whatever peanut butter was. Holly glanced around her room and couldn't see anything that looked edible, much less that could have been called peanut butter.

Natalie snorted. "You're being silly," she charged. "We have to go to the *kitchen*!"

Ah, the kitchen. But where was that? Fortunately, Natalie headed for the stairs, intent on showing the way.

The kitchen proved to be a white expanse of surprisingly alien territory, lurking behind the swing door at one end of the foyer. Gleaming gadgets with coiled electrical plugs lined the counter, there were stacks of dishes of every size within the cabinet door Holly opened, and a good dozen more cabinet doors lining the room.

Holly was overwhelmed. The occasional steaming mug of reindeer milk cocoa had never required so many tools to make.

But there wasn't even one reindeer in the carefully cultivated backyard and Holly wasn't quite sure how to proceed.

Natalie seemed to have no doubts. She opened a door in the front of a large white box—not without some difficulty—and stretched to her toes.

"It's back there. Unca Drew says it has to stay in the fridge because it's organic."

Holly was surprised to find the machine lit inside and full of all sorts of tempting tidbits. There was a jar at the back with a label which said "peanut butter."

Aha!

"I have to have milk for lunch, too."

Reindeer milk was good for little elves, so it made sense it was good for little mortals, too. Holly reached for the carton of milk, grateful she didn't have to hunt down those missing reindeer to milk them.

"I can help," Natalie insisted and pulled up a stool to the counter. She reached into a bag and pulled out two slices of bread, laying them flat on the cutting board. "You, too?"

Holly opened the jar and took a sniff. This peanut butter smelled wonderful! She nodded agreement. "We'll have lunch together."

Natalie began busily spreading butter on the bread, ready to make sandwiches—which was a good thing, because Holly knew nothing about the construction of peanut butter sandwiches.

It looked like she would have to learn.

OVER THE CRUMBS and empty milk glasses, Natalie met Holly's gaze. "What should we do this afternoon?"

What exactly did nannies do? Holly wished a bit too late that she had read her résumé before handing it over to Mr. Sinclair. It might have provided a few much-needed clues. "What do you usually do in the afternoons?"

"School," Natalie said with a little frown. "But Unca Drew said that I could stay home today to see the nannies. Tomorrow I have to go again."

"Hmm." Holly smiled. "Maybe we should take the chance to get to know each other a bit better."

Natalie's face brightened at the prospect, but she simply waited, her expression expectant. Holly suddenly recalled the little girl's delight with the earrings and had the perfect idea. "You don't have your Christmas decorations up yet."

The little girl's gaze slid away. "Unca Drew said he didn't have time," she admitted in a small voice. Natalie shrugged as though indifferent, but Holly wasn't fooled.

And she wasn't amused in the least.

No *time* for Christmas! Of all the selfish excuses! What kind of a person would deny a child the joy of the holidays for the sake of his own convenience?

Holly had a sneaking suspicion that she had just

been hired by exactly that kind of person. After all, she had had to explain the meaning of the season to the man already.

Her first impression of Mr. Sinclair had been exactly right!

And that was not good news, Holly realized with dawning horror. Because if Drew Sinclair didn't believe in Christmas, would he even believe in love or marriage? Holly couldn't imagine that he would.

And if he didn't believe in *that*, why would he ever ask Katherine O'Neill to marry him?

Oh no! Faced with the distinct possibility of failure, Holly took a deep breath and squared her shoulders. Mr. C. had trusted her with the job, after all. Holly could do it.

Holly *had* to do it.

For Natalie.

And she would have to start at the very beginning. Holly got up from the table and collected the dirty dishes, fighting to hide her annoyance from a little girl she suspected was very perceptive.

"Fortunately, *we* have lots of time today," she declared with cheerful resolve. "Let's do the decorating, just the two of us. That way, your uncle won't have to worry about a thing." She winked at Natalie. "We'll surprise him."

Natalie frowned with unexpected concern. "But, we don't have any money."

Holly blinked. "Money?"

"We *need* money," Natalie insisted with a solemnity beyond her years. "Unca Drew didn't give you any."

That he hadn't.

Whatever money was.

The gleam of hope in the blue glance the little girl slanted through her lashes made Holly determined to find some. She wondered whether she could be so lucky that Mr. and Mrs. C had planned for this eventuality.

After all, that résumé had just been tucked inside her purse, just waiting. Could she have been so lucky to be granted a magic bag, one that conjured up anything she might need? Holly retrieved her purse and rummaged in it, hoping she looked purposeful. There were tissues, a few mint candies, a comb and a small leather folder with a clasp.

Nothing else. Holly's heart sank. This wasn't a magic purse, after all.

Just when she could have really used one.

Natalie peered into the purse with open curiosity. "There's your wallet," she contributed with a seriousness that Holly was beginning to associate with the child. When Holly glanced up, Natalie pointed to the leather folder.

Holly dug the wallet out and opened it, almost afraid to look. There was a slot along one side and she cracked it open enough to peer inside. A lot of pieces of green paper were neatly tucked in there, but before Holly could wonder, Natalie gasped.

"You have *lots* of money!" she said with evident awe. Then she raised shining eyes to Holly. "This could be the *bestest* Christmas ever."

Holly decided in that very moment that she would make it so.

She smiled. "Then, we'd better get started. This is a big house and there's a lot to be done."

Holly carried the dirty dishes to the sink and hesitated. There was no hand pump for water and no bucket. But, Natalie opened a door in the lower cabinet with the familiarity of habit and reached for the plates. Holly eyed the stainless steel interior dubiously.

Her charge evidently noticed her surprise.

"Don't you have a dishwasher?" Natalie asked, as though unable to imagine such a possibility. Holly shook her head, knowing she'd never seen such a contraption and instinctively distrusting whatever it might do.

Even without her influence.

"It washes the dishes for you," Natalie explained. Holly had never liked washing dishes and was fascinated. She had a good look from a few steps away, not wanting to tempt the machine to do anything bizarre.

"I thought *everybody* had a dishwasher." Natalie stacked the dishes inside as though she did it all the time.

She probably did. Natalie closed the dishwasher door and Holly braced herself.

But nothing happened.

Nothing at all.

And the kitchen was sparkling clean once more.

Holly could definitely get used to peanut butter sandwiches and dishwashers. In fact, the mortal world had definite promise—with the marked exception of Natalie's curmudgeon of an uncle.

Well, Holly would have him straightened out in no time at all. This house would be more festive than the North Pole workshop itself by the time she was done.

Drew Sinclair didn't have a chance.

IT HAD BEEN A MISERABLE DAY.

Drew was bone-tired. He supposed everyone had rough days, but he didn't like having one himself. As he drove home in the early winter darkness, tired from conference calls and confrontations, too late for a decent dinner, he had a sense that there was something missing in his life.

He still believed with all his heart in the initiative he had personally begun within the bank, even if it wasn't easy. Maybe *because* it wasn't easy.

Drew believed in lending to small businesses. He loved their enthusiasm, their dedication, their creativity. He liked making his bank a part of their success.

All the same, Drew felt a personal failure whenever a loan went sour. He didn't like making mistakes, and he didn't like being wrong.

Not one bit.

Not that he hadn't tried. He had worked like a dog the last two months to help this business succeed. The fact was that Drew couldn't solve O'Neill Leathergoods' cash flow problems alone.

But Drew didn't have to like it.

He also didn't like being told that something he had seen with his own eyes was "impossible." That's what the tech support guy at the office had said when he'd asked about his printer. Drew ground his teeth and turned the corner to his street, resolving to fix the damn thing himself this weekend.

It was especially irritating that he had missed dinner with Natalie tonight. Drew had felt guilty calling to tell Holly he'd be late—it was her first day, after all!—and he knew he shouldn't have been surprised to find her tone a bit frosty.

He certainly shouldn't have been disappointed.

After this poor start, Holly probably thought he was some kind of workaholic. That bothered Drew as much as being late did, although there was absolutely no reason why he should worry what the new nanny thought of him.

But it bothered him, all the same. He hadn't been able to stop thinking about the sparkle of her unusual eyes all day long.

All in all, Drew was *not* in a good mood as he pulled into the driveway. He sat for a moment and studied the house that he called home.

It didn't look very homey. In fact, it looked a bit austere. All those softening touches that made a house feel like a home just weren't Drew's forte.

Drew sighed and leaned back in his seat. He didn't like being single, he didn't like going to bed alone, he didn't like that there was no one he could talk to about whatever happened in his day. He certainly hadn't planned for life to work out this way.

But Drew had just never met the right woman.

And he sure as hell wasn't going to spend his life with the wrong one.

He gave his head a shake and reached for his brief-case. One bad day didn't make his whole life a wash. The emptiness in Drew was just in his belly. He had forgotten to eat lunch, after all, and it was late. Drew hefted his briefcase and trudged up the steps. Too bad he was too late to read Natalie a bedtime story and tuck her in. He grimaced and his mood soured a little more.

Those moments were precious to him.

Drew unlocked the front door of his home and halted before a wave of cinnamon, cloves and allspice. He took a deep breath of it and half-smiled. The scent conjured memories of himself and Greg racing into the kitchen after school to find freshly baked Christmas cookies.

But no one baked cookies in this house.

Especially Christmas cookies.

Drew frowned. What was going on? He pushed the door fully open and was stunned by the sight that met his eyes.

His tastefully conservative hall had been decked in cedar roping hung with big plaid red bows. The same festive garland wound its way around the bannister and up the stairs, candy canes and Christmas balls periodically hung on its length. The door to his office sported a wreath hung with brass bells and another fat red bow that Drew knew hadn't been there that morning.

None of this had been here this morning, and none of it had been dragged out of his basement storage. Drew's lips thinned. He set down his briefcase with a thud of disapproval and hauled off his coat, determined to get to the bottom of this before things got worse.

Because someone had been busily breaking the one inalienable rule of his household.

Drew had a very good idea who it had been. He should never have impulsively hired a nanny!

Drew stormed toward the kitchen, purpose in every step, and flung open the swing door. He saw Natalie in the nick of time and bit back his expletive, quickly swallowing another.

What was she even doing up at this hour? His whole household had gone to hell while he was at work!

"What in the heck is going on around here?" he roared.

Silence descended on the kitchen with breathtaking speed. Drew scanned the damage. The once gleaming spread of marble countertop was generously littered with half-finished popcorn strings. There were trees cut of green construction paper scattered everywhere, rows of sparkles and stars haphazardly glued onto them.

Some of the sparkles had stuck to Natalie, who was sitting at a stool on the other side of the counter, and an errant gold star clung to her cheek like a distinctive freckle. There was a smear of chocolate on her chin and she held a gingerbread cookie shaped like a heart in one hand.

Her expression was alarmed, her eyes fixed on Drew, but his argument was not with his niece.

It was with the faintly flushed nanny who held a steaming tray of cookies, her hands encased in oven mitts shaped like Rudolph's head. Holly had sparkles in her hair and flour across her sweater, but the laughter that had tweaked her ruby lips this morning was banished.

She looked even softer and warmer than she had this morning and was, without doubt, the most perfectly alluring woman Drew had ever found in his kitchen. He stomped down on his inappropriate response before it, too, could get out of hand.

Holly stared at him as if uncertain what he would do.

"I asked you what was going on," Drew repeated coldly.

Holly licked her lips, glanced over the kitchen, then summoned a defiant smile. "We're getting ready for Christmas," she declared, then squared her shoulders.

There was a glint in her wondrous eyes that told Drew she had already guessed that this would not go uncontested. He was forced to admire the fact that she held her ground and was apparently ready to fight for what she thought was right.

But Holly Berry was dead wrong.

And Drew was going to make sure she understood that.

Right now.

"We don't decorate for Christmas here," Drew informed her, his tone positively glacial. "Period."

A frown flickered across Holly's brow, but she lifted her chin. "Natalie said you didn't have time. I thought that she and I could take care of things today and we've made great progress..."

"I *make* time for the things that matter," Drew retorted. "And this isn't one of them." He glared at Holly, willing her to accept his house rule without further argument.

They'd had a full year without Natalie's nightmares, and Drew intended to keep it that way.

But the new nanny wasn't going to let the matter go.

"Not one of them! How can you even say such a thing?" Holly dropped the tray of cookies on the stove with a bang.

"We have one rule and one rule only," Drew retorted. "We do not celebrate Christmas."

"That's cruel!" Holly propped her oven-mitt-encased hands on her hips and her eyes flashed. The move accentuated the narrowness of her waist, the bit of flour on the end of her nose made her look far from a worthy adversary. "That's unfair and it's *wrong*!"

Drew had to admire how she stuck to her guns. He folded his arms across his chest and summoned his fiercest glare.

Holly was clearly undeterred. "Mr. Sinclair, I have to disagree with you on this. Surely, there's no harm in enjoying the spirit of the season..."

"There *is* harm. Plenty of it."

"Mr. Sinclair! You're being unreasonable!" Holly tossed off the oven mitts and closed the distance between them with quick steps. Her voice lowered in appeal. "Christmas is for children, Mr. Sinclair, it's a magical time of the year. Whatever your own memories are, think of what this means for Natalie!"

"I *am* thinking of Natalie!"

Holly paled and held herself stiffly. "That seems unlikely," she charged softly.

Drew shoved a hand through his hair, feeling like the Grinch in the act of stealing Christmas. But he had no choice.

"Get rid of it all," he said grimly. "Now."

Holly's eyes widened in horror and she backed away, as though he was the worst villain she had ever met. The way her eyes darkened told Drew that she did not think much of his attitude.

Or of him.

But he was doing this for Natalie! Drew took a step in pursuit, needing suddenly to explain everything, to make Holly understand the reason for his concern. He'd gone about this wrong, courtesy of his hellish day, but surely Holly would agree with him...

"Unca Drew!" Natalie wailed and Drew remembered—too late—that the reason for his concern was still in the kitchen.

How could he have forgotten that she was listening?

Drew turned to his niece, hoping that he could

somehow make this better. "Natalie," he said in a softer tone, "I think it's for the best."

Natalie's bottom lip trembled and her eyes filled with tears. "But, Unca Drew, I'm having fun!"

Drew's heart wrenched, but he couldn't let her have those nightmares again. He loosened his tie and squatted down beside his niece. "Punkin, I don't want you to be afraid..."

"I'm *not* afraid!" Natalie cried. "I like Christmas. And I *hate* that we don't have it anymore!"

And with that, she flung herself past Drew and ran from the room. He hung his head in defeat as her footsteps pounded on the stairs.

Oh, he had handled that well, there was no doubt about it. It had been a four-star kind of a day—and it wasn't getting any better soon.

"Afraid of what?" Holly demanded softly.

Drew glanced up to find the condemnation had melted out of her expression, to be replaced with curiosity. That alone made him feel a little better.

"Why on earth is she afraid of Christmas?" The uncertainty in Holly's words made Drew realize that she already cared about Natalie.

Holly had just tried to do something festive with a little girl, a little girl who otherwise would have every reason to be excited about Christmas. Holly hadn't known the single reason why that couldn't be.

She *couldn't* have known because Drew hadn't told her. It was his own fault for not explaining things this morning. Drew sighed, stared at the floor, and decided it was better late than never.

"Two years ago, my brother's house burned to the ground," he confessed flatly. Holly caught her breath, but Drew didn't even glance up. His chest was tight with the memory of that night, and what had come after it. "He and his wife were killed, but Natalie escaped with very serious burns."

Holly gasped softly, but didn't interrupt him.

Drew swallowed and resolutely kept his gaze on the floor. "It was Christmas."

"Oh, Mr. Sinclair. I am sorry." There was no doubt in Drew's mind that Holly's apology came from the heart. He glanced up and saw the dismay in her eyes. "I never imagined..."

"No, you couldn't have known." Drew pushed to his feet and shoved his hands into his pockets, feeling that familiar emptiness flood through him one more time. He had never talked to anyone about that night.

There had never been anyone to talk to.

Drew frowned, pushing his own wounds aside, and forced himself to continue matter-of-factly. "We don't have Christmas because I don't want to remind her of it all."

Holly crossed the floor quickly and laid a hand on Drew's arm. He felt guilty for treating her unfairly and wished he could just come home all over again.

"I'm sorry," he said quietly and stared at his wingtips. "You didn't know. I shouldn't have lost my temper."

Holly smiled. "Don't apologize for being protective of someone you love, Mr. Sinclair."

He did love Natalie. Drew found himself very relieved that Holly understood exactly what had made him angry. Her words eased Drew's conviction that he had screwed up every single thing that had come his way today.

Maybe hiring a nanny impulsively had been one thing that had come out right.

Holly turned to indicate the room as Drew glanced up hopefully. "Mr. Sinclair, if you had come in here a bit differently, you would have seen what a wonderful time Natalie was having. Look at all she's done today!"

At her urging, Drew did look.

This time, instead of seeing a broken rule, he saw all the hours Natalie had spent cutting out trees and sticking on sparkles. A lump rose in his throat when he realized that it had been a small helper who decided that chocolate sprinkles had to be on every single cookie.

"She said she missed Christmas and that you were busy," Holly said quietly. "I'm sorry, I thought you just couldn't be bothered, and it was so very important to her." She took a breath. "I just wanted to make her happy."

Had she been happy? Drew knew he had to ask the question—just as he knew Holly would tell him the truth. "Did she smile?"

Holly shook her head minutely, then frowned. "A couple of times, I thought she might, but she never did." She looked into Drew's eyes with concern. "Does she? Ever?"

"Not since that night," Drew admitted and felt better just having the opportunity to voice his concern. He had no one to ask, no one with whom he could compare notes, and children certainly didn't come with instructions.

Surely if Drew had been a good enough "father" to Natalie, she would have smiled *once*?

Holly leaned closer, her silver eyes shining reassurance. "None of us can erase the past, Mr. Sinclair, but we have to go on to the future. Natalie *is* healing."

Drew frowned. "I'm not so sure."

"You should be, Mr. Sinclair. It says a lot that Natalie's ready to have Christmas again, and she is." Holly paused for a telling moment.

She tilted her head to watch his response to her next softly uttered words. "But the question is, are you?"

Drew scowled and surveyed the kitchen once more. It seemed very important that he answer Holly honestly. But he simply wasn't sure how much of his anger had been protectiveness of his niece and how much had been his own pain resurfacing.

Finally, Drew shrugged and met Holly's unswerving gaze. "I don't know." He ran a hand over his hair. "I just don't know."

Holly smiled, a soft smile that seemed just for him, and Drew felt a little less empty inside. Her fingers tightened on his arm and he was suddenly very glad that she was here.

His worries seemed a little less daunting, now that he had voiced them.

"I'm sorry that I didn't know the whole story sooner, Mr. Sinclair. Believe me, I would never have surprised you this way."

"I do believe you." As soon as he uttered the words, Drew knew they were true. Their gazes held for a long moment that awakened a tingle of awareness within Drew. He eyed those fragile fingers against the navy of his suit, the softness of those lips that could not seem to stop smiling, the bright intellect shining in those silver eyes.

He wondered suddenly what it would be like to kiss Holly Berry.

Drew frowned at the inappropriateness of his

thought. "I should go to Natalie," he said gruffly and stepped away.

But Holly's allure did not diminish with distance.

"Give me a moment with her," Holly suggested easily. "Take off your jacket and have a cookie." Her smile broadened. "Mr. Sinclair, Natalie will be just fine." Holly exuded such certainty that Drew actually believed her.

Not only that, he found himself tentatively smiling back.

"Call me Drew," he said impulsively.

Before he could wonder what had gotten into him, Holly's smile widened and a dimple made an appearance in one cheek. Drew was sure he'd never seen anyone so pretty in all his life.

"Drew, then," she said and wrinkled her nose playfully.

Drew liked the sound of his name falling from those red lips. Holly winked and brushed past him, calling "Natalie!" as she darted up the stairs.

Her light footfalls echoed on the hardwood floor overhead as Drew looked around the kitchen once more. The funny thing was that familiar ache inside him didn't seem to be quite so hollow as usual.

Nor nearly as big. In fact, Drew thought he *would* have a cookie. They smelled awfully good.

And they *were* good. Drew leaned against the counter, loosened his tie, and let a deluge of memories tumble through his mind as he chewed. He let himself think of Greg, of snowball fights on the way home from school, of a thousand precious moments, and found himself smiling at a memory of his brother for the first time in two years.

Drew treated himself to another cookie, shaking his

head at someone's diligence—and he could guess who—in providing the snowman with eyes, nose, mouth, eyebrows, ears and hair.

All in chocolate sprinkles. These were probably the most enthusiastically decorated cookies Drew had ever eaten. But he ate a second and a third, all the same, savoring their taste as well as the care with which they had been made.

And as Drew stood in his unusually chaotic kitchen, he had a sudden thought. Maybe, just maybe, Natalie wasn't the only one who had been missing Christmas around here.

THREE

HOLLY LEANED around the door jamb and watched her tiny charge sniffle. She was humbled by the concern she had seen in Drew's eyes and felt horrible that she had so impulsively jumped into a situation that she didn't understand.

He wasn't cold-hearted—he was very protective of a vulnerable child. Holly found herself admiring her new employer for that.

It seemed her talent for making a muddle of things was getting even worse.

"Natalie," she murmured softly, hoping she could make this right. The little girl sat up at the call, clutching a very well-worn teddy bear to her chest, as though he would protect her from harm.

She looked balefully at Holly. "You made Unca Drew mad," she accused.

"I did." Holly nodded and stepped into the room. She put her hands in her apron pockets. "I'm sorry, Natalie. I made a big mistake."

Natalie hugged her bear tighter and Holly thought a change of subject might be in order. "Who's that?"

To Holly's relief, Natalie brightened. "It's Mr.

Bumbles. He's my bestest friend in the whole world." She pulled back and fiddled with the bear's paw for a long moment.

When she finally continued, her voice became so quiet that Holly had to bend down to hear her words. "Sometimes, Mr. Bumbles has bad dreams about the fire."

Holly guessed that Mr. Bumbles hadn't had nightmares alone and only now understood the fullness of Drew's concern. She couldn't blame him in the least for being angry.

"Oh, that's terrible," she said quietly. "I sometimes have bad dreams, too, so I know how he feels."

Natalie looked up. "You do?"

Holly nodded. "It can be pretty scary."

Natalie looked back to the bear. "When I was little, I used to have bad dreams, too, but not anymore."

"Good for you."

"It's coz of the magic chair."

Holly's eyes widened in surprise. She didn't realize that mortals knew how to work magic. "You have a magic chair?"

"Uh huh." Natalie pointed to an old white rocker in the corner of her room. It didn't look very magical to Holly, but you could never be sure. "When I had my bad dreams, Unca Drew would come and I would sit on his knee in the magic chair and he would tell me how it would make all my bad dreams go away." She lifted her chin proudly. "And they did, just like Unca Drew said."

With that, the last of Holly's harsh judgment of Drew melted away. There were a lot of elves in this world who wouldn't have been so thoughtful of a child's fears, never mind busy mortals.

Holly perched on the side of the bed. "You're very lucky. Magic chairs are hard to find."

"I know." Natalie nestled closer to Holly. "If you have a bad dream, you can come and use my magic chair. I don't mind."

"Oh, that makes me feel much better." Holly smiled at this unexpected offer. Her determination to see Natalie's Christmas wish come true doubled. "Thank you."

Holly leaned toward the little girl and put a tentative hand on Natalie's shoulder. To her relief, Natalie snuggled in close. "And if you ever want anyone to sit in your magic chair with you, or with Mr. Bumbles, you can call me," Holly murmured. "It doesn't matter when."

Natalie looked up, then nodded. "Okay. But only if Unca Drew can't come. He knows how to make it work best."

Holly's heart twisted. Could she possibly have misjudged Drew any more than she had?

Low words from the hall interrupted Holly's thoughts.

"Maybe we could finish those decorations together this weekend."

Holly looked up to find Drew leaning in the doorway. He had loosened his tie and discarded his jacket. His chestnut hair was tousled and his eyes weren't quite as shadowed as they had been in the kitchen.

He really was quite an alluring mortal. Holly's mouth went dry. The corner of Drew's lip pulled hopefully, his gaze dancing between her and Natalie, and he almost smiled.

They were a pair, these two, with their hard-won

smiles! Holly fervently hoped that Drew had overheard Natalie's insistence on his magic chair competence.

"Finish them?" Natalie echoed as though she were afraid to hope.

Her uncle nodded firmly. "If we don't finish them, how can we hang them up?"

"We can hang them up? Really?" Natalie erupted from the bed and crossed the room in a flash. "Really? Can we? We don't have to get rid of them?"

"Not if you don't want to."

"I don't want to!" Natalie crowed with delight.

She latched on to Drew's leg and hugged him tightly. When he crouched down beside her, Natalie smiled.

Holly saw Drew's eyes widen, saw him try to hide his astonishment so he didn't startle his niece. His gaze flicked to meet hers and Holly let her delight show in her own smile.

Drew cleared his throat and tousled Natalie's hair with one affectionate hand. "Maybe we should have Christmas again this year," he suggested.

Natalie's approval of that was more than clear. "I already wrote Santa!"

"You did. I hope you've been good."

She smiled again. "Mr. Bumbles said so." Natalie's response should be more than enough to reassure Drew that his niece truly was ready for Christmas again.

"Well, then," Drew said sagely. "We can't have Santa coming to a house that isn't ready for Christmas. Good thing Holly's here to help." When Natalie hugged him tightly, Drew winked at Holly with a playfulness so unexpected that her heart skipped a beat.

A most alluring mortal indeed.

And it wasn't just his smile.

Drew's voice lowered as he set Natalie on her feet and his gaze rose once again to meet Holly's. "I'm sorry I got mad, punkin."

The light in his eyes told Holly that this apology was for her, too. She felt herself flush a little bit at the warmth in Drew's gaze and smiled at him, hoping he understood that she understood.

His response had been perfectly reasonable.

Natalie nodded, then bounced Mr. Bumbles on her uncle's knee. Her mind was clearly on more important matters than apologies. "Can we hang the decorations in the kitchen? Can we? And some more in the hall? Holly liked those plant ones, but I wanted to make some *special* decorations. Can I, Unca Drew, can I?"

"Sure." Drew's grin flashed at his niece's enthusiasm. He tapped a fingertip on her nose. "You can do anything you want."

That smile made a curtain call. "I'll make the very bestest one of all for your desk, Unca Drew!" Natalie punctuated her declaration with a wet kiss on his cheek.

Drew's smile flashed more broadly than it had thus far and the tension eased out of his shoulders. Holly's heart did its thumpity-thump and showed no signs of stopping soon.

"You've got a deal, punkin. Christmas is back." Drew stood and propped Natalie on his hip. His manner turned serious as he held up a finger. "But we've got to have one rule that no one can break, okay?"

Drew impaled Holly with a look that told her not to cross the line he was going to lay down.

She nodded mute agreement to whatever his terms might be. If nothing else, Holly already knew Drew would be fair and his request would be justified.

"No lights," he said firmly. "All right?"

Natalie seemed untroubled by this demand and Holly quickly acquiesced.

Drew winked at her, then frowned with mock sternness at his niece. "Isn't it awfully late for you to be up? Tomorrow's a school day, after all."

"But I had my bath!"

"I can tell." Drew wiped the smear of chocolate off Natalie's chin with one strong fingertip, his smile wry. "And what did you have for dinner?"

"Peanut butter sandwiches. Holly makes the bestest ones."

"I'll bet she does," Drew said softly.

To Holly's surprise, her new employer's gaze landed on her. The way he smiled directly into her eyes made Holly feel very feminine. And there was a funny tingling in her belly.

Never mind the pounding of her heart.

She obviously wasn't used to mortal men. Or maybe this strange feeling was just because she was relieved.

That must be it! After all, Holly didn't have to thaw out Drew Sinclair—which meant she could move right along with making Natalie's wish come true.

First thing tomorrow morning, Holly was going to find Katherine O'Neill. The good news was that she wouldn't have to be up half the night washing up the mess from making those cookies.

Because Natalie had shown Holly the dishwashing machine.

THE NEXT MORNING, Drew did something he couldn't remember ever having done before.

He overslept. It was true that he and Holly had taken a while to clean up the kitchen after Natalie was in bed—just as it was true that Drew hadn't rushed the process.

A kitchen couldn't be too clean, after all.

It was also true that Drew had found himself thinking about a certain intriguing nanny long after he should have been asleep. He told himself that he was just impressed that Holly had so quickly coaxed a smile from Natalie.

She had a gift, but her success also made him re-consider his own choices. Holly's arrival had shown Drew that maybe he hadn't been quite playful enough with Natalie. Playing wasn't something that Drew did instinctively—in fact, it had always been Greg who started their snowball fights.

Maybe it was time he lightened up.

Of course, he had only stayed awake so late to ef-fectively plan a strategy for that course of action. His inability to sleep hadn't had anything to do with a cer-tain pair of silvery eyes or a very kissable smile.

That wouldn't have been logical.

The sound of Holly's laughter in the kitchen was what finally awakened Drew that morning. He smiled and stretched leisurely as he opened one eye to glance at the alarm clock.

Drew saw the time, swore, and lunged for the shower.

In record time, he was trotting down the stairs, thanking the powers above that it was Casual Friday. Drew glanced in the hallway mirror on his way past and straightened his collar, feeling oddly nervous about stepping into his own kitchen.

He opened the door just in time to hear Holly's question.

"What would you think if your Uncle Drew got married?"

He froze on the threshold and watched as Natalie considered the question. The pair were apparently unaware of his arrival. Natalie was already dressed in her favorite denim pinafore for school and perched on her stool to watch Holly at work. Holly wore jeans that showed her slender curves to advantage and a red sweatshirt embellished with dancing candy canes.

It looked like Holly was making peanut butter sandwiches again. Drew stifled a smile. Maybe she couldn't cook.

Since Drew loved to cook, that was a flaw he could live with.

Or maybe he could teach Holly.

It would take a very long time, Drew was certain. These things had to be practiced, over and over again.

"I would have a mommy then," Natalie said finally.

Holly wrinkled her nose in the playful way that Drew was starting to find very sexy. "Well, not exactly. An aunt."

"But Unca Drew is my new daddy, so she would be my mommy."

Holly smiled, maybe at the same ring of conviction in Natalie's tone that made Drew smile. "But what would you think of that?"

Natalie nodded with vigor. "I'd like it."

"Maybe someone should ask what Unca Drew thinks of that," Drew interjected. Holly pivoted and flushed, her guilty response making Drew wonder why she was even asking such a question. Her gaze met his and flicked away, her blush deepening in a most interesting way.

Could Holly possibly be interested in *him*? Drew's pulse quickened as he watched Holly flush.

"We're having peanut butter sandwiches!" Natalie informed him, unaware of any adult subtext.

Drew raised his eyebrows. "Again? You're going to start to look like a peanut." He crossed the room and peeked under her pinafore, as though afraid of what he would see. When he saw she was wearing her striped green leotards, he made a face. "Oh! Remember the picture of the peanut plant in your book? You've got little roots just like it!"

Natalie squealed and examined her legs, her expression turning tolerant. "Unca Drew, those are just the lines on my leotards."

"Phew!" Drew wiped his brow in mock relief.

"You're silly." His niece giggled, the sound making Drew catch his breath. He looked to Holly and she smiled encouragement in a way that made him feel giddy and young again.

Then Holly bit her lip. "You don't usually eat peanut butter sandwiches for breakfast?"

"No." Drew tousled his niece's hair. "I think you've been getting biased information."

Natalie grinned and bit into her sandwich. "Holly likes them, too."

"For breakfast?" Drew had to ask.

Holly flushed again as she nodded, then an enchanting smile curved her lips. She was definitely a woman challenged on the culinary front. Imagine, living on peanut butter sandwiches!

Natalie would be in seventh heaven.

"Once in while, I guess it can't hurt." Drew accepted the sandwich Holly offered and took a bite. "You know, you were right, Natalie," he said a moment later. "Holly does make awfully good peanut butter sandwiches."

Holly looked self-consciously pleased. "It's not that hard..."

"Ah!" Drew lifted a finger. "Don't be giving away your secrets," he teased, then winked at her.

Holly not only smiled, she laughed out loud. Then she winked at Natalie. "Your uncle is teasing me," she informed the little girl, who beamed at them both.

"He only does that to people he likes," Natalie declared.

Holly's glance flew to Drew and he felt the back of his neck heat. "Don't worry about dinner tonight," he said as casually as he could. "I'll cook."

Holly's eyes widened.

"Don't look so surprised." Drew pretended to be insulted. "I'm a man of many talents, right, Natalie?"

"Unca Drew cooks nice food."

Holly looked skeptical at this endorsement, then her lips quirked as she met Drew's gaze again. "Peanut butter sandwiches?"

Drew laughed in turn. "Not a chance. Chinese food."

Holly looked suitably surprised. It wasn't a common thing to do, Drew knew. "I went to cooking class once," he explained. "Szechuan and Cantonese 101. I thought it would be a great place to meet interesting women." Holly arched a questioning brow and Drew's lips twisted at the memory. "So did the other sixteen guys in the class."

Holly's dimple appeared. "There were *no* women?"

Drew shook his head. "Not a one. Evidently, they were down the hall in Small Engine Repair." Holly laughed and he shrugged. "It wasn't such a loss. I still meet a couple of the guys for racquetball once in a while." He winked. "We compare brands of oyster sauce."

Holly's eyes continued to shine in a most intriguing way, but unfortunately Drew couldn't linger here all day. He glanced at his watch and grimaced. "Do your best at school today, Natalie."

"Uh huh. You do your best, too, Unca Drew." Natalie slipped off her stool to give Drew a sticky kiss goodbye.

"I'll try." Drew found his gaze rising to meet Holly's. "You'll do your best, too?" he murmured and she grinned.

"I'll try."

Drew nodded and made for the door, pausing halfway there to glance back, hoping against hope that he could sound nonchalant. "Oh, and Holly, I think marriage is a great idea. Always have. I just never found the right woman to share it with."

Their gazes held for an electric moment and the stardust in hers seemed to shimmer. Drew wanted to sit right down at the kitchen table and spend the entire day talking to Holly instead of reviewing loan applications and business plans. He wanted to watch her smile, he wanted to make her laugh, he wanted to give her that kiss.

Drew knew that if he didn't leave right this minute, he wouldn't be able to leave at all.

Tonight couldn't come soon enough, to his thinking.

At least, it was the beginning of a weekend. Drew consoled himself with that thought—and immediately tried to think of a way to convince Holly to spend her off days with them. He waved and left the kitchen quickly, well aware of Holly's gaze following him.

DREW WASN'T aware of his niece's gasp of delight—even less the little half-smile of anticipation she kept to herself.

That little girl was quite certain she had just had a glimpse of something she wasn't supposed to see.

Natalie was quite sure she had just caught a glimpse of a special Christmas secret that Santa was making just for her. She couldn't imagine how she would wait for Christmas Day.

Because it was clear to Natalie Sinclair that Santa was reading his mail and checking it twice.

Good thing she'd been nice.

Holly opened the dishwasher and made a face at all the dirty dishes still there. "You said it washed the dishes," she charged.

Natalie bounced across the room and pointed to the little dish inside the door, more than willing to explain. She liked Holly. A lot. And she especially liked what Holly was going to *be* on Christmas Day.

It wasn't Holly's fault she'd never had a dishwasher.

"You have to put soap in there and then you close it —" Natalie demonstrated "—and you turn it on with this button." She fixed her nanny with a serious glance. "But you have to wait until it's all the way full, coz Unca Drew says so."

Holly nodded, then peeked inside once more. "It's not full yet," she decided and Natalie had to agree. Holly wrinkled her nose and smiled in that way that made Natalie want to smile back. "We'll let it do its magic tonight."

"Okay." Natalie skipped off to get her coat to go to school, convinced that Santa was bringing her the bestest Christmas gift ever.

She had a feeling that Unca Drew was going to think so, too.

NATALIE INTRODUCED Holly to her teacher, a lovely mortal with golden skin, then ran off to play. Ms. Monteray had eyes so dark they seemed to go on forever and her manner was so tranquil that Holly was certain she had just met a being of rare wisdom.

After all, Ms. Monteray was a *teacher*.

Knowing a teacher was a good thing because Holly had a real problem.

She didn't know how to locate Katherine O'Neill. Maybe Mr. C. had engineered this encounter, as well.

"It's a pleasure meeting you, Holly," Ms. Monteray said smoothly. "I'm glad Mr. Sinclair found you so quickly. Will you be meeting Natalie at noon?"

"Oh yes, I'll be here." When the teacher nodded and might have stepped away, Holly blurted out her question. "Do you know Katherine O'Neill?"

Ms. Monteray repeated the name, then frowned. "No, I don't think I do. Should I?"

"I don't know. I need to find her."

"Ah!" The other woman smiled. "You're supposed to look someone up. Are you new in the city?"

Holly nodded.

"Don't you have a phone?"

Holly shook her head.

"Well, there's a telephone book in the office." Holly's confusion must have shown, because Ms. Monteray pointed to the building entry. "Right through there, turn right, it's a black door on the left. Ask Marianne for the telephone book."

Holly thanked the teacher so profusely that the woman looked a little alarmed, then dashed off as bidden. The office was a small drab room in the precise location Ms. Monteray had specified.

"Can I help you?" A silver-haired woman perched before a humming machine glanced up over her glasses. Her expression wasn't very welcoming.

"Are you Marianne?" The woman nodded but otherwise did not move. "I'm Natalie Sinclair's new nanny. Ms. Monteray said I could ask you for the telephone book."

The woman's chilly demeanor thawed slightly. She got up, retrieved a thick book and dropped it on the counter between them with a thump. She didn't appear ready to relinquish it. "Who are you looking for?"

Holly silently sighed with relief. It was no small thing to have assistance with unfamiliar things. "Katherine O'Neill."

Marianne flipped open the book and fanned through its pages. Holly was amazed by the thin white paper, no less by the tiny type that covered each page. Elvish vision was clearly going to be an asset here.

She squinted and realized that each column sported a name linked to a sequence of numbers. It must be a magic code!

Ms. Monteray was indeed wise to send her this way.

Marianne spread the book open on the counter and ran her fingertip down a column. "Here. O'Neill. Oh, it says to check O'Neal and O'Neil." She peered over her glasses. "Do you know which way it's spelled?"

"No."

"Hmmm." Marianne pursed her lips. "Do you know whether it's Katherine with a C or with a K?"

"No, I don't."

Marianne rolled her eyes and pushed the book towards Holly. "Well, then, you've got a lot of phoning to do. There are fourteen C. O'Neill's, twelve K. O'Neill's, three C. O'Neil's and four K. O'Neil's." Marianne smiled primly. "You're lucky. There were no C. or K. O'Neal's."

"Oh." Holly scanned the listings and realized that Marianne was right. She must have looked particularly dejected, because the woman reached over and patted her hand.

"It won't take that long, dear."

"I don't have a phone," Holly confessed, remembering how that had surprised Ms. Monteray.

Marianne's brows rose. "There's something different. Here, you can use the office phone." She patted a black device sitting at the end of the counter.

It was clearly a machine.

Holly licked her lips and felt an inkling of dread. What would go wrong when she touched this phone?

She hesitated and Marianne cleared her throat with a trace of her earlier cold manner.

"Honestly, you'll never get finished if you don't get started." She marked the first possibility with her fingertip, picked up the crescent-shaped part of the black phone and put it to her ear. "You've got to dial a nine first," she said matter-of-factly, then poked the button marked "9".

Marianne said the numbers out loud from the book and poked them into the machine in sequence. "There. It's ringing." She handed the crescent-shaped part of the phone to Holly.

Holly mimicked her gesture and held it to her ear. She just had enough time to be confused by the periodic ringing that came from the device before things got much, much more confusing.

Every single phone in the office began ringing simultaneously. Marianne jumped in alarm, but before she could pick up even one, they stopped and started again. Within moments, the office was filled with a cacophony of phones starting and stopping intermittently, each screaming for attention. There was even one chirping from Marianne's purse.

It was enough to make Holly want to cover her ears. She could hear more phones ringing throughout the rest of the building. She strained her elvish hearing and discerned the ringing of phones in the houses that surrounded the school. She heard more phones with different ringing sounds, probably in purses and pockets. It seemed every one of them had come to life simultaneously.

Just as suddenly as it had begun, the noise stopped.

The office seemed eerily still after all that ruckus.

Even the phone Holly held made no noise at all anymore.

Marianne picked up the phone on her desk, listened and frowned. "There's no dial tone. Something's gone wrong with the service."

Holly had a very good idea what that was.

Or at least, who was responsible.

Marianne pulled a smaller device from her purse, tapped at it and scowled. "Even my cell phone doesn't work!" she declared.

Holly tried to look sympathetic.

Marianne muttered something unflattering about telephone companies and Holly took the chance to thank her. She scurried away from the school guiltily, wondering how on earth she could fix whatever she had done.

Let alone how she was going to find Natalie's new mommy.

DREW FOUND himself watching the clock all afternoon. For the first time in a long time—perhaps ever—he couldn't lose himself in the business plans piled on his desk.

His thoughts kept wandering back to the memory of a pair of silvery eyes.

And precisely what he would make for dinner. He wanted to impress Holly with his cooking. It had been a long time since he'd been looking forward to a woman's company this much. Drew skipped out early to go to the market, the vision of the meal crystal-clear in his mind. He arrived home in record time and practically bounced up the steps.

The wreath on the front door of the house made him smile—Holly and Natalie had been busy again. Drew could see his niece's hand in the glitter glopped onto the pine cones and an artistic sense he was beginning to associate with Holly in the clustering of those cones.

They made a good pair.

That thought made his smile broaden. Drew juggled the groceries, managed to pull out his keys, and got the door open without dropping anything.

"I'm home!" he called, unable to explain the lightness that had taken his heart hostage.

Drew kicked the door closed just as Holly came from the kitchen. She seemed to be deliberately avoiding his gaze, but before Drew could ask what was wrong, Holly tilted her head toward his office.

"Someone's here to see you," she said softly. Her gaze flicked to his and Drew caught a glimpse of unexpected concern. He stepped forward, wanting to solve whatever was bothering her, but Holly simply lifted the groceries out of his hands and stepped away. She looked to the office pointedly once more before disappearing into the kitchen.

Drew frowned, then turned to find the last person he wanted to see waiting in his office.

Katherine O'Neill rose elegantly to her feet, her reddened lips curving in a smile Drew could only call predatory. As always, her suit was impeccable designer fare, every hair was in place and her accessories were of the finest Italian leather.

Of course.

"Drew!" she chided as though they were more intimate than they ever had been. "Tsk tsk! You haven't been returning my calls."

FOUR

DREW WAS ready to nip this visit right in the bud. "What else do you expect when you default on your loan? It's too late for excuses, Katherine. We've been around and around on this." He noted with satisfaction that her smile faltered ever so slightly. "It's out of my hands now."

"But, Drew, I'm certain we can work something out!"

"I'm not." Drew deliberately did not step across the threshold of his office.

"I am," she breathed. Katherine's smile turned sultry and she stepped close enough for him to catch a waft of her perfume. She was so polished, as perfect as a magazine model, that Drew wondered whether there was anyone real behind the carefully-maintained façade.

She fingered his sleeve. "Why don't you and I go for dinner?" she purred. "Just to discuss the possibilities. I've made a reservation at my favorite little French bistro and we can have a less formal chat." She wrinkled her nose but the gesture didn't look nearly as sexy as when Holly did it.

The reminder made Drew impatient to get into the kitchen and the evening he was looking forward to. "I have plans."

Katherine arched a brow. "Dinner at home with the child and the nanny?" Her disapproval was more than clear, her own objectives becoming more clear as her fingertips walked up his sleeve. Her voice lowered. "Come for dinner, Drew. Come play with the adults."

Drew shook off her touch. "We've nothing to talk about, Katherine. We've spent the last two months trying to put a package together that would work and you've missed every single commitment. It's over."

Katherine lifted one brow. "Unless I can come up with a payment for the bank," she mused.

Drew folded his arms across his chest. "But you don't have the cash. You know it and I know it. That's it, Katherine. They won't play any more."

"Even if I get a personal endorsement?"

Drew's lips thinned. "At this point, you need cash."

"A loan, then," Katherine murmured with a seductive smile. "A quiet little loan from a very personal friend." Her fingertips traced circles on his sleeve and she leaned closer.

Drew finally realized what she meant. He stepped back in horror. "I'm not lending you any money!"

Katherine pouted. "But, Drew..."

"But nothing! Katherine, you're out of line." Drew couldn't believe her nerve. "After what just happened with that loan, how can you imagine that I would *personally* lend you any money?"

"Drew, it wouldn't be much and it wouldn't be for long," Katherine practically begged, her eyes wide with appeal. "Just three months, then my receivables will come in and there'll be the increased sales over the holidays..."

"Followed by the retail doldrums in the winter. Forget it, Katherine." Drew shoved a hand through his hair. "I can't believe you're even asking me this."

"It wouldn't be much. Just fifty thousand dollars."

Drew choked on that number, but Katherine rushed on. "I know you can afford it, just look at this place. It would be nothing to you and everything to me."

She gripped his arm and stared deeply into his eyes. "Drew," she whispered, "you have the power to make my dream come true."

It seemed rather pedestrian that the dream at the root of this performance was a leather-goods store.

Drew shook off her grip. "I said no." He gestured to the door. "As I mentioned, I do have plans for this evening."

Katherine straightened, brilliantly playing the role of the wounded innocent, one betrayed by a trusted ally. She even managed to summon a tear of disappointment, presumably for his lack of faith.

Drew wasn't impressed.

"I could make it worth your while."

Drew opened the door.

Katherine's bottom lip trembled. "It's the only thing I ever wanted," she confessed unevenly. She reached for his sleeve. "That is, besides..."

But Drew didn't care about Katherine's dreams. "Then you should have managed the books better and kept your word, instead of spending money that wasn't yours to spend," he charged quietly. "Goodnight, Katherine."

Katherine inhaled sharply and Drew thought her eyes flashed. She spun and snatched up her fur coat, then marched to the door with less than her usual grace.

But by the time she met Drew's gaze, her eyes were softly luminous and he wondered if he had imagined her anger.

"I can't believe you've become so cold-hearted, Drew," she whispered. Her lashes fluttered to her cheeks and before Drew could fathom what she was going to do, Katherine stretched to her toes and pressed a kiss to his cheek.

"Think about it, Drew, please." She raised one hand and touched his chin as Drew stared at her. "For *me*." Katherine's hand trailed to his chest, her eyes filled with tears, but Drew held her gaze steadily.

"No," he said quietly, expecting more of an argument.

Instead, Katherine pivoted to leave suddenly, so suddenly that Drew hoped she'd accepted the truth. He shook his head, locked the door and headed for the kitchen.

Enough business already. It was time to get cooking. He pushed up his sleeves and strode into the kitchen with an expectant smile.

HOLLY COULDN'T EXPLAIN her lousy mood. She had spent most of the day unsuccessfully seeking Katherine O'Neill and despairing that she could fulfill her mission.

Yet when this gorgeous mortal showed up at the door and introduced herself as the woman in question, Holly hadn't been glad to see her.

Not in the least.

It must be because of Natalie. After all, Holly had a hard time imagining that this woman was mommy material. The way Katherine turned up her nose at the sight of Natalie and instructed Holly to keep the "brat" away from her had been a big clue.

When Drew strode into the kitchen with a red lipstick kiss on his cheek and a smile on his lips, Holly knew that the way her heart sank to her toes had nothing to do with Natalie at all.

IT WAS a relief for Drew to step into the warmth of the kitchen and put Katherine and her visit behind him. She was so typical of the women he met, all polish and insincerity, expensive dates each and every one.

Holly, though, was completely different. In the wake of Katherine's visit, Drew realized that was part of what had intrigued him about Holly from the very beginning. She seemed so natural, so sweet and giving, so unlike self-motivated women like Katherine.

Drew liked that very much. Natalie launched herself across the room to give him a big hug and he scooped her up to swing her around. Drew snuck a glance at Holly to find her features pale and her eyes averted.

What was wrong?

"You've got icky stuff on your face," Natalie accused.

Drew ran his fingers over his cheek and they came away adorned with red lipstick. He rolled his eyes, swallowed something unflattering about Katherine, and tore off a paper towel. He scrubbed and presented himself to Holly for inspection. "Gone?"

She didn't smile or meet his eyes, but simply shook her head.

Drew rolled his eyes, unwilling to leave the kitchen so soon after he had arrived. "Can you get it for me?"

Holly wet the paper towel and scrubbed off the lipstick with quick gestures. The move brought her close and Drew smiled as the scent of her skin wound into his nostrils. He was fiercely glad to be home—and determined to convince Holly to spend the weekend with himself and Natalie.

Even if she still wouldn't meet his gaze.

Something *was* wrong.

Holly lifted her hand away and forced a prim smile. "All gone." She would have moved away but Drew captured her hand in his and pulled her to a stop.

"What's wrong?" He ran his thumb across Holly's palm, instinctively liking the soft smoothness of her hand in his. "Did something happen today?"

Holly licked her lips and flushed. "Nothing important."

"Tell me," he urged softly.

Holly flicked a glance up at Drew. "Well, I *did* break the phones at the school," she admitted quietly, as though fearful of how he would react.

Drew frowned, not certain he understood, but Natalie was ready to supply details. "All the phones went off, all at once, when Holly took me to school."

"When I touched one," Holly clarified dejectedly.

She had touched a phone the moment the system

went down and thought herself responsible. Drew's lips twitched despite himself. "But you didn't do it," he assured her and squeezed her fingers.

"Oh, I think I did."

It was hard to fight his smile, but Drew saw that Holly was convinced of her own guilt. "Holly, that's impossible. You're blaming yourself for something completely out of your control. Phones *do* stuff like that."

A hopeful light dawned in Holly's eyes and Drew caught his breath when she gazed up at him. "Really? Often?"

"Well, no," he had to admit. "Hardly ever, actually, but it happens." Drew smiled for her and pulled her a little bit closer. "You couldn't possibly have been responsible for it."

"Oh." That seemed to reassure her slightly.

Anxious to take advantage of the moment, Drew found himself speaking with uncharacteristic haste. "Holly, I was wondering what your plans were for the weekend." She looked perplexed. "You know, Saturday and Sunday should be your days off and if you have any plans, I certainly would understand, but I was wondering whether you'd like to spend some time with Natalie and I."

"I have no plans," Holly conceded and Drew grinned.

"Well," he said, forcing himself to sound stern. "We have a very serious problem and it might just be the kind of thing you could help us with."

"We have no problem," Natalie declared loyally.

"Oh, yes we do, punkin. Have you seen that living room of ours?" Both nanny and child looked blank, and Drew leaned closer to Holly as he lowered his voice. "I'm certain it's missing something, but I'm not sure what it is." He pursed his lips. "Something big and green with shiny stuff all over it."

"A Christmas tree!" Natalie squealed. She dove off her stool and danced around the end of the counter. "We're getting a Christmas tree. Holly, you *have* to help!"

To Drew's relief, Holly didn't look dismayed at this possibility.

In fact, she lifted a warning finger for Natalie. "But no lights," she reminded the little girl, her silvery gaze rising to meet Drew's.

His heart began to pound in a most erratic manner. "We'll have to go out to a tree farm because the very best Christmas trees are the ones you cut yourself," Drew said and pulled a newspaper clipping from his pocket without releasing Holly's hand. "It just so happens that there's one not too far away." No one had to know how long he'd looked to find it. "One with sleigh rides, I'm afraid."

"With horses?" Natalie's eyes went round.

Drew nodded. "With jingle bells." He grimaced. "Probably a lot of candy canes, too. Christmas cookies."

"And reindeer milk cocoa?" Holly breathed.

Drew laughed. "Well, cocoa of some kind." He gripped her hand tighter. "Will you come?"

Holly smiled so warmly that Drew's uncertainty dissolved. "I'd love to." Drew stared into the shimmers of Holly's eyes and was quite certain there was nowhere else in the world he wanted to be. Her lips parted ever so slightly and that inappropriate urge to kiss her came back with a vengeance.

Then, Natalie interrupted the course of his thoughts. "Who was that icky lady?"

"Someone from work." Drew was dismissive. "She shouldn't have come to the house."

Holly flushed in a most flattering way and actually fidgeted. "She said the phones were out when she tried to call beforehand."

This time, Drew couldn't stop his chuckle. Holly fought her own smile, but lost the battle, her dimple finally coming to light.

"I don't like her," Natalie asserted, and stuck out her tongue as though that conclusion wasn't clear enough. "And she didn't like me neither."

Holly clicked her tongue disapprovingly, but Drew spoke up. "Well, she's gone now, punkin. What do you say we start dinner?"

Natalie glanced up. "Holly lets me help," she declared archly, an obvious reference to Drew's usual method of cooking alone.

But Drew just grinned. "Well, then," he sighed with mock concession, "I guess I'll have to make room for two helpers tonight." He glanced to Holly, sensing her uncertainty. "If you want," he amended and won another bone-melting smile.

"I'd like to learn," she admitted shyly and Drew knew everything was going to be just fine.

CHICKEN IN BLACK Bean Sauce was much, much more interesting than even peanut butter sandwiches. Not to mention that Cantonese Chow Mein. Drew was clearly a master at this cooking business.

Although, it seemed that he had used every single pot and dish in the kitchen. Thank heavens for the marvel of the dishwasher. Holly lay in bed and patted her full belly, admitting that mortals and their ways could certainly grow on an elf.

Or more specifically, Drew and Natalie were growing on Holly.

But soon, Holly would be leaving. Soon, Katherine O'Neill would move into this house and Holly would be on her way northward. Disappointment coiled within Holly but she knew it wasn't justified.

Katherine had kissed Drew, after all, and Drew had smiled about it. So, the romance was on track and Holly was doing her job.

Then, why did she feel so irritable about it? Maybe this was what success felt like—goodness knew Holly had virtually no experience with it.

But that didn't seem quite right. Holly frowned and watched the stars. She liked how she could lay on the bed and see the stars through the overhead skylight in her room. It was very peaceful to simply lay here through the night and watch the stars dance around while the mortals slept.

Of course, Holly was spending a lot of that time thinking about one particular tall and handsome mortal with a very engaging smile. She sighed and refused to worry about Katherine for the moment.

Fact was, Holly liked Drew better without his suit —he looked less dauntingly formal—she liked when his hair was more disorderly and his eyes sparkled with mischief. He seemed more playful each time she saw him, and his antics as he cooked tonight had made Holly laugh out loud more than once.

She liked Drew Sinclair.

She didn't like Katherine O'Neill.

That was the meat of the matter. Holly frowned.

But it wasn't up to her. She had been sent to do a job and by all appearances, it was getting done. Maybe she should just trust Mr. C.'s instincts and enjoy the fact that everything— for once in her life—was going according to plan.

In one short week, she'd be back at the North Pole.

The prospect seemed a bit flat. Holly sighed. She chewed her lip, wishing she knew what Drew really thought of Katherine. Did he know something about this woman that Holly didn't? It wasn't an unlikely possibility.

Holly swallowed, remembering the seriousness in his eyes when he had asked whether she could spend the weekend with the two of them. She hadn't anywhere else to go, but Holly knew that wasn't the reason she had agreed.

She wanted to know more about Drew Sinclair. In the darkness of her room, Holly admitted that it wasn't so that she could make sure he married Katherine O'Neill.

But no one else had to know that, did they?

DREW DREAMED OF OCEAN WAVES. They rolled in from the horizon and pounded on an endless beach in rhythmic succession, they roared and foamed and lapped against his toes, and dripped.

Dripped?

Drew woke suddenly, the unmistakable sound of incessant dripping in his ears. His dream dissolved into the familiar silhouettes of the furniture in his bedroom, but the dripping didn't fade away.

He sat up and frowned, but the sound didn't stop. If there was a leak, he'd better find it now. He tugged on a sweatshirt and track pants and stepped out into the darkened hall.

The Little Mermaid nightlight glowed orange from the electrical socket by Natalie's room, the rest of the hall was shrouded in shadows. Drew could hear the gentle rhythm of his niece's breathing.

Punctuated by that relentlessly steady drip.

Drew listened. Definitely not the bathroom. And not from the third floor. It might be coming from the kitchen. He trotted down the stairs, strode down the hall and flung open the kitchen door for the second time that night.

The suds surged forth to embrace his legs and rolled into the foyer.

Drew surveyed the kitchen in shock. The room was knee-deep in soapsuds. They frothed over the counter from the sink. The dishwasher churned merrily away, no doubt making even more. That steady drip echoed in the room and he wondered just how much water had leaked into the basement.

He waded through the foam, and turned off the dishwasher. It fell silent as though reluctant to do so and Drew surveyed the damage.

He could make a good guess what the problem was. Drew opened the cupboard below the sink, eyed the relative positions of the contents, and knew exactly what Holly had done.

It wasn't the first time it had happened here. Drew's lips twisted in recollection.

The dishwasher chose that moment to inexplicably spew one last volley of rinse water into the overloaded drain. Suds exploded out of the drain and rained down over Drew like big snowflakes. They spread across the kitchen counter. The geyser even splashed the ceiling.

By the time it stopped, Drew was not only soaked to the knees but dappled with water everywhere else. It was a hell of a way to wake up at—he looked to the clock on the stove—1:14 in the morning.

And the worst thing was, he couldn't stop himself from chuckling. He leaned against the counter, tipped his head back and laughed out loud.

HOLLY HAD HEARD that dripping and had hoped desperately that it hadn't been anything wrong—or more importantly, anything wrong for which she could be deemed responsible.

She had a funny feeling that Drew wouldn't be as understanding about her foibles as even Mr. C. had been. Holly chewed her lip and waited, her dread rising with every moment. Until suddenly, she heard the unmistakable sound of Drew Sinclair.

Laughing.

Holly sat up in the darkness, confused. She listened again, but there could be no mistake.

He was *laughing*. Even though something was still dripping.

Holly couldn't deny her curiosity. She slipped from the bed, crept to the top of the stairs and listened. Gradually, she moved to the first landing, then the second. The deep sound of Drew's laughter made Holly's own lips tug.

But what was so funny?

She moved down to the foyer and any tendency to

laugh was immediately dismissed. The golden light from the kitchen was spilling into the hall—along with a considerable quantity of soapsuds.

Holly bit her lip and remembered the printer. And the school phones. She should have known that the mortal world would be a veritable minefield for her.

She figured she might as well get the worst behind her. She took a deep breath and stepped into the suds, putting herself in clear view of the man in the kitchen. Drew's laughter slowed to a chuckle as he eyed her.

The grey sweatpants he wore were wet and clung to his muscled thighs in a way that was decidedly distracting. His faded red sweatshirt emphasized the breadth of his shoulders, the opening at the front revealed a little bit of very masculine chest hair. His hair was rumpled, his eyes twinkling and Holly had a very hard time concentrating on what she had to say.

"I'm sorry about the mess, Drew," she said quietly and he sobered. "I just have this thing..."

"This thing?" Drew leaned against the counter and looked as though he was fighting against a smile.

And losing very badly.

Holly cleared her throat and stared at her interlaced hands. "Yes. It's terrible. You see, machines just don't like me."

Drew said nothing, no doubt as he came to terms with this enormous flaw. If Holly's pointed ears hadn't been safely concealed, she knew they would have been glowing red.

She cleared her throat and continued. "It's very embarrassing, but I can't do anything about it. Machines just take one look at me and go crazy."

Holly flung out her hands, more than a little disconcerted by Drew's silence. "In fact, it's awful. Mrs.

C. said that I have a gift, but I don't think so, not at all. It's always the same. And there's nothing I can do!"

"Oh, I think there is." Drew folded his arms across his chest as Holly watched. To her surprise, even in the wake of her confession, there was an undeniable thread of humor in his low voice. He arched a brow. "You could, just for example, not put the liquid dishwashing soap into the dishwasher."

Holly blinked. "I don't understand."

"Obviously." Drew snorted, but there was a teasing glint in his eyes. Holly stared at him, unable to explain his response. "Holly, you have to use the special dishwasher soap because it doesn't foam as much. Didn't you see the box?"

"Um." Holly licked her lips. "No."

Drew grinned. "It's a mistake anyone could make, especially if it's all new to you." Holly was so astounded that she could have made a forgivable blunder that she didn't know what to say. "I did it myself once, a long time ago, and my brother never let me forget it."

Holly could barely wrap her thoughts around that astonishing admission.

Drew had made such a mistake?

But he did *everything* right! Holly felt a sudden and very strong alliance with this mortal, who otherwise appeared to be different from her in every conceivable way.

And she did like how he smiled.

"You?" she echoed incredulously.

Drew smiled right on cue. "Oh, yeah. I was worrying about something else and grabbed the wrong box." He shook his head and rolled his eyes. "Unfortunately, there were witnesses. You should have *heard* Greg."

Holly instinctively knew that he referred to Natalie's father, the brother who had died.

"I mean, he was the one who was always getting into a muddle," Drew continued. "He just loved that I had finally screwed up, and in such a big way. It gave him something to tease me about for years. He actually accused me of having done it on purpose to make sure the kitchen was *really* clean."

Holly smiled at the affection in Drew's tone. "You must miss him," she ventured and Drew's smile immediately faded.

"I do." He looked around the kitchen, eying the suds, and frowned thoughtfully. "I really do."

"Why don't you tell me about him?" Holly suggested, startled at the speed Drew's gaze locked with hers.

Then his eyes darkened. "I'd like that," he said huskily. "I'm guessing that you're a good listener, Holly Berry." The conviction in his low voice made Holly's heart skip a beat.

Then it skipped another just for good measure. The kitchen suddenly seemed very warm as the two of them stared into each other's eyes.

Holly decided she must be very, very unaccustomed to mortals. Or maybe all elves felt this way around men.

Or maybe, it was time she got this floor cleaned up and stopped staring into a certain man's eyes. Holly stepped forward with purpose.

Then slipped in the suds.

Holly squealed, Drew called her name and jumped forward. He caught her around the waist, then slipped himself. They went down together, in a flurry of arms and legs and soapsuds, and landed with a thump.

Holly was in Drew's lap, his arms around her waist, her breasts pressed against his chest. There were soapsuds on the side of her face and she could feel the dampness soaking through her clothes. She was very aware of the muscled thighs that had kept her from landing on the floor.

Then she made the mistake of looking up.

And Holly was aware of nothing beyond Drew's warm gaze. Holly's pulse began to echo in her ears when he lifted one strong hand to gently wipe away the suds that adorned her cheek.

"Not your color," he teased and Holly felt herself flush.

She caught her breath as Drew studied her features, a wonder dawning in his expression that Holly knew couldn't be associated with her. She was just a perfectly average and slightly unlucky elf, after all. But Drew's slow smile made her tingle right to her toes.

"You have the most amazing eyes," he murmured. "And you always look like you're ready to smile." The warmth of his fingertip slid across her lips as though he couldn't stop himself from touching her and Holly had a sudden—and very unelvish—urge to have this man touch more than her lips.

She impulsively reached out and mimicked his gesture, running her fingertip across his firm lips. His eyes darkened, then he captured her hand in his. The way Drew cradled her hand in his made Holly feel very tiny and feminine, though all of this was very new to her.

Drew pressed a kiss into her palm, his gaze unswerving from her own. Holly's eyes widened at the shiver that rolled over her skin from that one featherlight touch.

Maybe mortals did understand something about magic, after all.

Or maybe just this one did.

Holly watched, breathless, as Drew slowly leaned closer. It was as though he was afraid she would pull away, but Holly had no intention of going anywhere. He paused, his lips a finger's breadth away from hers, his gaze searching. Holly understood that Drew was waiting for her agreement to continue.

So, she smiled.

Drew smiled back. He eased the last vestige of suds from her cheek, then his hand slid along her jaw and into the hair at her nape, awakening an army of tingles along the way.

Holly had never felt anything quite like this. Drew placed her hand on his chest and Holly was astonished to feel his heart thundering at the same accelerated pace as her own.

They had more in common than using the wrong detergent in the dishwasher. Holly caught her breath.

Drew whispered her name, then his lips brushed across hers. Holly closed her eyes as starlight sparkled through her veins and she leaned a little bit closer.

Drew needed no more encouragement than that. He gathered Holly against his chest, his strong arms encircled her, his mouth slanted over hers with purpose. Holly felt safe and secure within his embrace, cherished and admired in a way she never had before. She understood as Drew kissed her just how special this man's protection could be.

Rather inconveniently, she thought of Katherine in that very moment. Holly broke away from Drew's kiss and bounded to her feet, leaving him looking more than a little astonished.

It was Katherine, after all, who was destined to be protected and cherished by this man. "You were going to tell me about your brother," she said hastily.

Drew got to his feet more slowly, his gaze steady upon her. "I will," he said solemnly, then half-smiled as he brushed the suds from her sweatshirt with a deliberation that made Holly's heart skip again. "Why don't we clean this up, first?"

FIVE

DREW AWAKENED to the enthusiastic bounce of his niece on his chest. "Unca Drew! It's snowing!"

He opened one eye and grinned at Natalie's delighted smile. One glance toward the window revealed big fat flakes wheeling out of the sky. "Looks like a good day to find a Christmas tree," Drew declared and Natalie gave him a kiss.

He wiped at the residue on his cheek. "Let me guess. Holly made breakfast."

Natalie giggled and nodded. Then she squirmed off the bed, heading for the kitchen and, no doubt, more peanut butter.

The change in his niece was amazing and it was all because of Holly. Drew rolled out of bed and headed for the shower, unable to keep himself from whistling. Even he looked happier. He winked at his reflection and conceded that Holly was working her magic on everyone in this household.

Drew had been amazed at how much he had told her the night before about Greg. It seemed that once he started talking, he hadn't been able to stop. Two years of holding back his grief hadn't diminished it in the least.

Holly, lovely Holly, had patiently listened to it all. Just sharing his burden had diminished its weight beyond belief—and in the wee hours of the morning, Drew had found himself eating Holly's Christmas cookies and even telling her about those old snowball fights.

Holly had helped him work past the painful memories to the good ones. It was the most wonderful Christmas gift anyone could have given Drew—that and Natalie's rediscovered smile.

It paid to be patient, Drew decided. He had waited a long time to find the right woman to share his life and had found a woman more right than he ever could have expected.

It was time, Drew informed his reflection, to start building some new good memories. He had a very strong feeling that Holly Berry was the one he should be sharing them with.

HOLLY HAD NEVER IMAGINED that finding a Christmas tree could be such fun. She refused to worry about the fact that Katherine apparently wasn't going to be joining them and forced herself to believe that her mission was on schedule.

It was hard to be anything but happy in the company of these two mortals. The tree farm was a delight, the snow absolutely perfect. A pair of massive horses, their harnesses jingling merrily, hauled the sleigh out into the fields as all the mortals aboard sang Christmas carols.

It reminded her of celebrations at the North Pole, but with mortals instead of elves.

Holly loved it.

Drew swung Natalie on to his shoulders when they set out in search of the perfect tree, to ensure that she had a good view. It took a long time to make a choice, what with the snowball fights that kept erupting and the angels Natalie had to make in every expanse of snow.

By the time they dragged their tree back to the sleigh stop, Holly suspected she wasn't the only one thinking longingly about peanut butter sandwiches.

The little shop by the parking lot had cocoa and cookies, to her delight. There were even a few reindeer, although they weren't inclined to confide their names in Holly. She did ask politely, much to her companions' mutual amusement.

Reindeer could be testy, Holly knew, particularly this close to their big shift of the year.

Drew lingered in the shop on their way to pay for the tree and Holly wondered what was taking him so long. She retraced her footsteps, Natalie trailing behind, and found Drew frowning at a box of several hundred tiny white fairy lights.

He must have heard her coming, because he spoke without looking up. His tone was thoughtful. "Holly, do you think I'm being too tough about the lights?"

Holly bit her lip, not entirely sure why he was so adamant about them. "You seem to feel pretty strongly about it."

Drew flicked an intense glance her way. "The fire

was started by a short in the Christmas lights," he confided in an undertone.

That fire. Holly eyed Natalie, who was more interested in reindeer made of clothespins than any adult conversation. All the same, she took a step closer to Drew. She still didn't completely understand. "What's a short?"

Drew rubbed his brow. "When the wires rub together wrong. There were mice in the attic—they'd chewed the electrical wires in the lights." He grimaced. "Actually, in a lot of the house."

"Oh." Holly peered at the box. "Have these been chewed by mice?"

Drew's smile was fleeting. "No. Of course not."

"Are there mice in your house?"

"No."

Holly met Drew's concerned gaze. "And the wire in your house?"

"I had all the wiring replaced when I bought it." This time, Drew's smile lingered a little longer. "Just to be sure. You can't be too careful, you know."

Holly smiled back at Drew, understanding that he was referring to his own cautiousness. Then he turned the box slowly in his hands and cleared his throat. "But maybe I'm being a bit too careful about this," he mused. He impaled her with a glance. "What do you think?"

Holly had to be honest with him. "I cannot understand—if all the wires are new and there are no mice—how there could possibly be the same problem."

Drew slowly smiled. Holly loved how gradually his expression changed, how he could summon a smile from the depths of serious consideration. She felt like she was watching a sunrise.

"You're right, Holly," he agreed warmly. "I'm being

too cautious again. And what's a Christmas tree without lights?"

"It would still be a Christmas tree."

"But not as pretty a one." Drew's gaze flicked over Holly's head and his smile widened. A mischievous glint lit his eye. "Look!" he murmured. "You're standing under the mistletoe."

Holly only had a moment to look and see that he was right before Drew kissed the tip of her nose. A few people near them applauded and laughed, then Natalie tugged at Holly's sleeve.

"Me, too!" she demanded and Holly bent to kiss the little girl's cheek under Drew's watchful gaze.

"Now, then," Drew said with mock ferocity. "Don't we have some serious decorating to do?" Natalie cheered, Drew winked and Holly couldn't help but smile.

She liked how Drew took Natalie's hand in his, put her own hand in his elbow, and led them to the cashier. She blushed furiously when the cash registers immediately started to malfunction, spewing tape and adding everything up wrong, but everyone else took it in stride.

In fact, the clerk confided with a smile that she preferred to add things up by hand. "Better for the old noggin," she declared and Drew laughingly agreed.

Holly just tried to keep a low profile until they were safely out of there.

BY MONDAY NIGHT, Drew knew the truth. He was smitten, and he wasn't going to fight it.

He whistled as he strode through the underground

from his office to the parking garage, knowing he hadn't felt so optimistic in years. They had had a great week-end, real family stuff, the kind of close camaraderie he'd missed the last two years. Natalie had been as busy as a bee with her decorations and the tree was virtually overwhelmed by her efforts.

They had made popcorn garlands and eaten a good part of the stock. Holly had made perfect little bows for the pinecones Natalie had rescued from the backyard. They had gone tobogganing on the fresh snow and stopped for latte and cocoa on the way home.

The most precious part of all was that Drew and Holly had already developed a routine of sitting in the kitchen after Natalie went to bed. Holly never seemed to get tired of talking or of listening, she always was ready to laugh. Drew had taught her to play Scrabble—and Holly had promptly beaten him.

All in all, it had been an absolutely perfect week-end. The thought uppermost in Drew's mind was how to ensure they had many, many more of them. He no-ticed a Christmas display at a florist's shop and paused to buy a sprig of mistletoe.

Natalie's reaction to him kissing Holly at the Christmas tree farm had been everything Drew could have hoped for. In fact, Holly was everything Drew had ever hoped for in a partner. She was clever and playful, she had a sense of humor, she was warm and giving, she cared deeply about Natalie's welfare. Be-sides her physical attractions, there was a sincerity about Holly that deeply appealed to Drew—he knew instinctively that she would always tell him the truth.

Drew Sinclair was falling madly in love for the first time in his life and he didn't care who knew it. Holly made him feel lighter, made him laugh more, made him concentrate on what was really important.

He had called home twice today—for no good reason at all—just to hear her voice. Drew had even left early tonight—just so he could get home and see Holly again.

Yes, he was definitely smitten. Drew grinned, took his acquisition, and headed for the garage.

He could only hope this feeling was mutual.

It might be time to find out.

HOLLY WAS NOT NEARLY SO convinced that things were going to plan by the time Drew came home Monday night. In fact, it seemed to her that Katherine O'Neill should have been around some time over this weekend if Drew intended to propose to that woman in five short days.

It also seemed to Holly that Drew shouldn't have been kissing her with such enthusiasm if he was going to marry someone else.

Also, she was quite convinced that she shouldn't have enjoyed those kisses at all.

But Holly had.

She covered the bread with peanut butter, biting her lip when Drew called from the foyer. Natalie danced out to meet him, her Christmas poster for his office finally complete.

It was a drawing of Mr. C. himself, lavishly adorned with sparkles and sequins, in the very moment before he dove down a chimney. His reindeer pranced behind him on the roof, impatient as they tended to be.

Holly had helped Natalie write each of their names above them. It was snowing and the sky was filled with very large stars. Natalie explained that Santa was holding a finger to his lips "shhhh" so that no one woke up the children.

In big letters of her own, Natalie had written BE-LIEVE above the entire scene. Holly listened as Drew admired the marvelous drawing, then the pair's voices faded as they went into his office.

No doubt to find the perfect place. Holly smiled despite herself at Drew's obvious love for his niece, and the two came into the kitchen before she could completely dismiss her expression.

"Aha! What's Holly smiling about?" Drew teased.

"Peanut butter sandwiches for supper, that's what," Natalie affirmed with obvious anticipation.

Drew soberly regarded the sandwiches Holly was making for dinner, but the twinkle in his eyes belied his expression. "I think"—he said with utmost seriousness —"that we'll have to seriously consider expanding your culinary repertoire." He arched a brow as his gaze locked with hers. "Over the long term, of course."

Holly's breath caught in her throat. Here was her chance to find out what he was really thinking, although she had a hard time forcing the words from her throat. "Won't Ms. O'Neill want to cook herself?" she asked in a strained voice.

Drew frowned. "What?"

"Ms. O'Neill. When she moves in," Holly's voice faltered, but she forced herself to continue. She buttered bread with a vengeance, unable to completely blink away her disappointment. "Surely she'll have plans of her own."

"I'm sure she does, but they have nothing to do

with me, or you, or Natalie, or certainly with moving into this house." Drew's words were resolute.

They didn't? Holly slanted a glance to a very watchful Natalie and took precisely too long to come up with her next question. "But..."

"But, obviously you've been working too hard," Drew murmured, intent glowing in his eyes. "Making sandwiches. You need a little relaxation, Holly." He paused and she caught a glimpse of mischievous twinkle in his eyes. "Maybe some Christmas decorating."

Drew stepped closer and conjured a familiar piece of greenery from a shopping bag. "Any ideas where we should hang this? Oh! How about right here?"

Holly knew what Drew was going to do the barest instant before he did it. But when he flicked the mistletoe over her head, Holly couldn't escape because of the counter beside her.

She couldn't argue because his lips were locked on hers.

At least that was what Holly told herself as she closed her eyes and leaned into Drew's kiss.

DREW EVENTUALLY HUNG the mistletoe in the foyer and he had been diligent in catching Holly each and every time she passed beneath it. She had to be honest with herself and admit that she quite enjoyed the way he kissed her, the way he held her, the way his touch made her heart skip in an uneven kind of way. She liked talking to him, she liked how delighted he was when she surprised him.

The fact was, though, that Holly wasn't here to kiss Drew Sinclair. She wasn't even here to fall in love with this tough and tender man, which was what she was pretty sure was happening. No, sir. Mr. C. had entrusted her with a mission and Holly had to see it done.

After all, she couldn't stay here forever. She was an immortal elf, and immortal elves belonged at the North Pole workshop. And Holly wasn't going to be allowed back there unless she succeeded. What she needed was a little job security—and that could only come from getting Drew to marry Katherine, regardless of what he thought of the matter.

In four very short days.

Desperate times called for desperate measures. As soon as Natalie was safely at school the next morning, Holly raced back to the house and pushed up her sleeves. She had to get Katherine back into the picture —because Drew clearly wasn't going to do it.

Holly had an awful feeling that that had been a "farewell forever" kiss she had seen on Drew's cheek.

She had to work fast! Holly practically ripped the house apart that morning, looking for some reference— *any* reference—to Katherine O'Neill. She poked through the files in Drew's office, she rifled through the papers neatly stacked on his desk. She pitched order into chaos, wanting only to solve this problem.

Shortly before lunch, she found it.

Katherine's name was written on a little card attached to a row of other similar cards, apparently organized alphabetically. Below was inscribed *O'Neill Fine Leathergoods* in decisive handwriting that had to be Drew's own. Holly ran a fingertip across his script, then frowned. Immediately below Katherine's name was an address and telephone number.

Holly knew better than to touch the phone. She memorized the address and resolved to find it this very afternoon, once Natalie was safely back at school.

There wasn't a moment to waste.

KATHERINE O'NEILL WANTED to sit down and weep.

But she couldn't, because the movers would have just trampled right over top of her. They were here at the behest of the bank, doing their job in laying claim to everything of value inside her shop. Every dream she had ever had was walking out the door and there wasn't a damn thing Katherine could do about it.

But she had worked so hard! It wasn't fair.

Damn Drew Sinclair and his bank anyway.

Left with no other options, Katherine stood in the corner, folded her arms across her chest and sulked. In fact, she was so busy feeling sorry for herself that she barely noticed a slender dark-haired woman slip through the doorway and scan the shop.

When the woman smiled tentatively and headed for Katherine, the former shop owner bristled at the interruption. She glared at the approaching woman and realized she was a vaguely familiar if rather plain woman.

The woman smiled.

Katherine did not. "Do I know you?"

"Oh, yes. I'm Holly Berry."

That meant just about nothing to Katherine. "We're closed," she snapped. "As if you can't tell."

Katherine turned away, wanting only to brood over her misfortune in privacy.

"No, you don't understand. I'm not here to buy anything. I'm Natalie Sinclair's nanny, but I have a mission to fulfill." Katherine's ears perked up at the mention of that familiar surname and she glanced back to find the woman blushing. "That is, I've come to get you."

"Me?"

The woman cleared her throat. "I know that you have a certain affection for Drew, I mean for Mr. Sinclair."

"What are you talking about?" Katherine demanded.

"Just that I've been looking for you. That you and he..." The woman frowned and swallowed awkwardly. "Mr. Sinclair said he was very interested in marriage."

That got Katherine's attention. "To me?"

The woman's cheeks pinkened again. "To the right woman, he said."

Katherine clutched the woman's sleeve. "When? Precisely when did he say this?"

"On...on Friday."

"Ha!" Suddenly, Katherine's future seemed much brighter. She had seduced reluctant men before and she would do it again. Although she never would have imagined that Drew Sinclair would be anything but blunt about his feelings on any matter, this cast a very different light on matters.

Obviously, he was just playing hard to get. And she, foolish trusting Katherine, had thought him disinterested in her many charms.

Apparently, she had retreated from the game too early.

So, Drew had sent a message. The wily devil.

Katherine set to thinking. Imagine, if she married Drew, her shop could be a little joint venture. In fact, all that lovely money Drew refused to lend to her would be half *hers*.

At least, it would be when she got him to sign a nice little prenuptial agreement. Katherine nearly rubbed her hands together with glee. She'd have fine leather goods stores all around the globe!

They'd throw roses in Italy when she arrived to spend her semi-annual budget in Milan. She'd dine with all the famous designers and have each and every one begging at her slender feet for her endorsement. She'd make and break manufacturers by whim alone.

She would be the queen she deserved to be.

It was all within reach.

"Stop!" Katherine cried as the movers hefted another box of perfectly divine ostrich evening bags. She pushed past Drew's messenger, intent on seeing results and the sooner the better. "Stop right there and put it all back," she commanded. "There's been a new development."

The head mover frowned. "But ma'am, we have instructions..."

"Forget them! I'll contact the bank myself."

The men, hesitantly, put that box of ostrich purses back down. It was but the first victory of many. Why, the tide was turning, even as Katherine watched.

What she needed was a plan. It wouldn't do to run straight to Drew. No, that would make her look *biddable*.

Katherine was anything but biddable. She really ought to get the legal agreements drawn up first. Yes! That would be a perfect strategy. Then Drew could sign before she finished seducing him, while he was still overwhelmed by her charisma.

Perfect! Katherine was so busy getting her lawyer on the phone that she didn't even notice a saddened Holly ease out of the store and run down Bloor Street.

HOLLY SIGHED and watched the clock that night. Both Drew and Natalie apparently noticed her mood, because they exchanged a concerned glance. They set as one to cheering her up—in fact, they were so thoughtful that Holly wanted to sit down and cry.

She knew, deep down inside, that Katherine would never appreciate this pair the way they deserved. Holly braced herself for the inevitable moment of that woman's arrival, trying to bolster her conviction that Mr. C. had it right.

But the minutes passed and Katherine didn't come.

Natalie demanded that Holly help tuck her into bed and even offered Mr. Bumbles to console her nanny. Holly did cry then, just one or two little tears, which her charge sweetly kissed away. Drew watched carefully from the hall and Holly couldn't meet his eyes when he eased past her to tell Natalie her bedtime story.

Holly sat in the kitchen and watched the clock tick as the low rumble of Drew's voice carried through the house.

Katherine still didn't come.

Holly was so busy puzzling over this that she jumped when Drew appeared. "Want to talk about it?" he asked quietly, but Holly shook her head.

She was quite proud of herself for managing to summon a smile. "It's not important."

"Hmm." Drew said and sat down beside her. Holly found her fingers captured within his hand and his gaze boring into hers. "You listen to me, I listen to you," he declared in a low voice. "That's the deal around here, okay?"

Holly shook her head but before she could protest, Drew laid a warm fingertip across her lips.

"No rush," he said gently. "But I'm here when you're ready."

Holly knew that Drew would always be there for anyone who relied upon him. That was one of the things she admired about him. He was so steadfast and protective, so gentle and yet strong. But Holly wouldn't get to rely on him, not after Katherine became his wife.

Not after Katherine became Natalie's new mommy.

Holly blinked back her tears and stared at their entwined hands, not having the will to pull her fingers away from Drew's. She had a feeling she was going to treasure this moment for a long time.

"Hey," he said softly and squeezed her fingers. "Why don't you beat me at Scrabble?"

Holly nodded agreement, grateful for anything that would take her mind off the scene ahead. Drew pulled out the board. Holly knew he would try to make her laugh and eventually, he did.

Even though Katherine still didn't come.

DREW DIDN'T KNOW what was bothering Holly, but he knew what was bothering him. His growing feelings for his niece's nanny were quite inappropriate under the circumstances.

He didn't think it was right to continue this way and he wondered if that was what was troubling Holly.

She must be wondering what his intentions really were. After all, she had asked about Katherine moving into the house, which was a laughably remote possibility.

But then, it wasn't laughable that Holly was concerned.

Drew didn't want Holly to have any doubts because he didn't have a single one. He paused before a jeweler's window in the underground, one whose work he had always admired, and eyed the rings displayed there. Drew shoved his hands in his pockets and considered the matter.

It wasn't like him to be impulsive. He'd only known Holly Berry for a week.

On the other hand, Drew had been looking for the right woman long enough that he figured he ought to be able to recognize her when she showed up on his doorstep.

He really didn't want Holly worrying about the future.

Impulsiveness did have its benefits. After all, Drew had hired Holly impulsively and she had made Natalie smile in short order. That was an encouraging thought.

Greg had always told Drew that he could stand to lighten up a bit.

Greg had also told him that he'd know the right woman for him as soon as he met her. That's how it had been with Winona. Greg had been a believer in love at first sight.

Holly had made Drew a convert.

He smiled at the recollection of his brother, decided his heart was probably going to keep skipping as long as he thought about Holly, and stepped into the jeweler's shop.

Drew intended to think about Holly for a very long time.

BY CHRISTMAS EVE, Holly was really worried. Katherine still hadn't come. When the doorbell rang in the late afternoon, Holly ran down the hall and practically flung open the door.

Holly was surprised that she felt no relief to see Katherine's cool smile or her elegant little black dinner suit. In fact, Holly was oddly disappointed to find the woman there at all—and even more disappointed to see Drew's car pulling into the driveway.

Holly swallowed. Her assignment was going to be done all too soon.

Katherine waved her red-leather-gloved fingertips. "Hello, Drew! What perfect timing."

"Katherine," Drew frowned and slammed the car door a bit more loudly than he usually did. To Holly's surprise, when he strode closer, it was clear he wasn't very glad to see their visitor. "What are you doing here?"

Katherine chuckled. "A little early Christmas present, Drew." She wrinkled her nose. "Just for you."

Drew grimaced. "I've heard all about the run-around you've been giving the auditors this week. It won't get you anywhere, Katherine, and I'd strongly advise you give it a rest." He flicked a glance at Holly and smiled, just for her. "Hi, Holly."

Holly's heart fluttered in response to his low greeting.

"Doesn't the *child* need you?" Katherine asked Holly pointedly.

The child in question poked her head around Holly, her hand gathering a fistful of Holly's skirt. Holly was struck by the way Natalie hovered behind her, exactly as she had lurked behind Drew just a week before.

"You're the icky lady," Natalie said bluntly. "Unca Drew said you shouldn't have come here."

Katherine's lips thinned. "Well, I am here and I'm back to stay."

"What?" Drew was clearly incredulous.

Katherine sniffed. "We've just had a misunderstanding, Drew, that's all it is. I know that you want me and I certainly"—she smiled with confidence—"want you. It's perfectly understandable that you'd prefer not to lend money to someone outside of your family."

Drew blinked but Katherine hauled an envelope from her alligator purse. "I've taken the liberty of having my lawyer draw up an agreement for our...merger."

"What merger? What the hell are you talking about?" Drew took the envelope with a frown, pulled out a document and scanned it. Horror dawned on his face. "This is a prenuptial agreement!"

Katherine smiled. "All standard and customary for

the modern wedding, my dear." She pointed to the bottom of the document. "You just need to sign right down there..."

"But I'm not marrying you!"

Katherine blinked. She glanced at Holly and gritted her teeth. "But *she* said that you were interested in marriage."

Drew's lips set grimly. "I am. To the *right* woman." He stepped onto the porch. "Sorry to be blunt, Katherine, but that's not you." He handed her back her document, took Holly's elbow and stepped into the house. "Goodnight, Katherine. Have a merry Christmas."

"You!" Katherine let loose a string of profanity, but Drew decisively shut the door in her face. He looked down at Holly and she had the distinct sense that she had mucked something up one more time.

Worse, this time, she had done a particularly good job.

Without a single machine in sight. It seemed that her abilities were expanding in a most disconcerting way. She swallowed carefully.

"Natalie," Drew said softly. "Can you go and color in the kitchen, please? Holly and I need to talk."

Oh, this was going to be bad. Drew looked very grim. This was a hundred times worse than being called into Mr. C.'s office.

Natalie scampered away, but Drew didn't loosen his grip on Holly's elbow. There was no escape.

"Holly, did you really have anything to do with that?"

Holly felt her cheeks burn and knew she couldn't possibly conjure up a plausible explanation in time.

She had to try. "Well, I thought when you talked

about marriage," Holly took a deep breath, knowing that wouldn't lead anywhere helpful and tried another tack. "Natalie would like a new mommy and I..."

"Don't worry, Holly," Drew said so confidently that Holly had to look up and meet his gaze. He smiled slowly. "I've found the perfect candidate."

Who? Holly was confused. There were no other women around and Mr. C. had said it would be Katherine.

Drew released Holly's elbow and pulled a small box from his pocket, a shred of doubt filtering into his eyes. He caught her hands in his and leaned toward her.

Holly braced herself for very bad news.

When Drew spoke hastily, she knew he wanted to get the worst over with as well. "Look, Holly, I know this has happened really quickly, but I don't want to continue on like this and have you worrying about the future."

"You're going to fire me," Holly whispered fearfully.

"No!" Drew shook his head. "Well, not exactly. That is, there's"—he hesitated and rolled the tiny box in his grip, then suddenly impaled Holly with a bright glance—"there's another job I'd like you to consider."

Drew put the little box into Holly's hands and folded her fingers around it. "This is for you," he murmured.

Holly took it because she didn't know what else to do. Drew was so serious. She certainly didn't understand. Holly nibbled her lip, eyed the gift, then decided she might as well open it. Maybe it was a farewell gift of some kind.

But inside the box, there was only a golden band nestled in the deep blue velvet lining.

Holly knew exactly what kind of ring it was. Her heart stopped cold and she stared at it, unable to believe even her keen elvish vision.

"Holly, will you marry me?" Drew said quietly. "I know we've only started to get to know each other, but I'm already falling in love with you." Holly glanced up with surprise. "I think it's only going to get worse," he confided with a tentative grin.

Holly couldn't help but smile back.

Drew seemed to find her response encouraging. "Holly, I want to spend the rest of my life learning more about you and laughing with you. I want to come home, knowing that you're here, I want to teach you to cook and talk with you all night. I want to catch you under the mistletoe when you're not expecting it, I want to let you beat me at Scrabble over and over again."

Holly gasped. "You did not let me win!"

Drew grinned. "Maybe just the first time."

Holly laughed out loud before the need to confess her fatal flaw made her smile disappear. "But, Drew, I'm always messing things up," she protested.

He smiled with an affection that couldn't be denied. "On the contrary," he said smoothly. "It seems to me that you've been very busy *fixing* things since you got here."

Well, she had brought Christmas back to this house. Natalie did smile now and Drew, well, Drew had lightened up in a most interesting way.

Maybe this was her *niche*.

Holly ran her fingertip across the ring and stared into Drew's eyes as a lump rose slowly in her throat.

Nothing would make her happier than to accept Drew's proposal. Seeing Mr. C.'s mission complete, even having a permanent job at the North Pole workshop, just couldn't compare to what she had found here.

The *only* thing Holly wanted was what Drew was offering. She wanted to stay in this house, she wanted to be his wife, his friend, his confidante, his lover. She wanted to be Natalie's new mommy more than she'd ever wanted anything before.

"I know it's sudden," Drew said urgently, as though he felt the need to convince her. He folded her hand into his. "But it's *right*, Holly. I know it and I hope you feel the same way."

Holly did feel the same way. She knew that this man was absolutely the most perfect companion she could ever have.

But no matter how much she wanted to do so, Holly knew couldn't marry Drew. He was a mortal and Holly was not.

Holly swallowed and looked down at the ring, wondering how on earth she would explain that to Drew.

Somehow she had to find a way to tell him the truth.

She parted her lips, but Drew silenced her with one fingertip. "Just think about it," he urged. "I don't want to rush you, Holly. I just want you to know that I'm serious about this." Drew smiled with rare uncertainty. "Just promise me you'll think about it until the morning."

Drew kept his fingertip pressed to her lips, as Holly nodded.

"I love you." Drew smiled into her eyes and Holly

decided in that moment that she wasn't going to just think about his proposal.

She was going to *do* something about the only thing that stood between them. It took a lot of gumption to ask for exactly what you wanted, but Holly now knew what that was.

Fortunately, she knew exactly who could make her only wish come true—and this was the night to ask.

SIX

HOLLY SAT beside the Christmas tree, watching all those little white fairy lights twinkle in the darkness. She had promised Drew that she wouldn't go to bed and leave the lights on, but Holly had no intention of going to bed.

She was waiting for someone.

And she would wait all night, if necessary.

When a distinctive prance sounded on the rooftop, Holly clenched her hands tightly together and once again rehearsed what she was going to say. There was a *poof* of ash in the fireplace, then a familiar grunt carried to Holly's ears.

Then a great jolly elf landed behind the brass fire screen with a resounding thump. Mr. C. shook out his hat and brushed off his jacket, hefted his sack and saw Holly.

He froze for a long moment. His red lips pursed and the apples in his cheeks dimmed ever so slightly. Mr. C. adjusted his spectacles and peered through them at Holly once again.

"Hmmm," was all he said.

Holly didn't need Mrs. C. to tell her that Mr. C.

wasn't pleased. She pushed to her feet and folded her hands in front of herself, but her little speech wasn't going to have a chance to be heard.

"You're still here," Mr. C. noted quietly.

"Well, yes. I mean, the job isn't done."

"Ah!" Mr. C. eyed the tree, the garlands, the decorations. He peered toward Drew's office and Holly knew that his elvish vision was as keen as her own. She could barely make out Natalie's picture, fastened in a place of pride, and knew she didn't imagine the little smile that curved Mr. C.'s lips.

It seemed to Holly that his gaze lingered on the mistletoe hanging from the foyer light fixture. She had the distinct sense it was tattling on what it had witnessed.

She blushed.

Mr. C.'s eyes twinkled so briefly that Holly thought she might have imagined it.

He pivoted abruptly, without saying anything, then moved deftly toward the Christmas tree, acting for all the world as though Holly wasn't even there. He cleared a space beneath the tree with businesslike ease, and deposited an array of parcels garbed in glittering paper.

Just when Holly was wondering whether he would even acknowledge her again, Mr. C. glanced over his shoulder. His twinkling gaze met hers and he deliberately winked.

When he turned to face her fully, Holly saw why.

Mr. C. was holding out a tiny parcel wrapped in shining gold paper. There was a golden bow that was much too large perched atop it. He held it out toward her and Holly's heart started to hammer.

"You might as well have your Christmas gift here

and now," Mr. C. rumbled, laughter hiding in the depths of his voice.

"For me?"

"Are there any other elves named Holly Berry here?" Mr. C. looked so pointedly under the furniture that Holly had to smile.

"But I didn't even ask for anything."

Mr. C. smiled and his dimples danced. "Didn't you?" he mused.

Holly looked into his eyes and suddenly understood. "You knew!" she breathed.

"Holly! How could I do this job if I couldn't hear the secret whispers in every heart?" He leaned closer and tapped a gloved finger over her own heart. "Even elvish ones?"

Holly knew that was true.

She accepted the parcel, which was lighter than a feather in her hands. She was dying of curiosity to open the box, yet afraid it contained something other than the only thing she really wanted.

She met Mr. C.'s gaze. "I love him."

That smile broadened, something about it making Holly want to smile in return. "I know." Mr. C. nodded. "Didn't Noel say you would find your place?"

Holly shifted the parcel from one hand to the other, trying to compose one last appeal. She was sure it couldn't be very easy, even for Mr. C., to give her what she wanted. "But, Mr. C..."

"Holly," he interrupted sternly. "Open it."

Holly took a deep breath and did what she was told. She tore off the bow and ripped open the paper.

Only to find that there was nothing inside the wrapping at all.

Holly gasped and looked to Mr. C., whose smile

did not waver. "Wish, Holly!" Mr. C. advised. "You have only to *wish* for your heart's one desire."

"I want to be mortal," Holly said without hesitation, just uttering the words not seeming to be enough. "I want to be mortal!" she said more loudly. "I want to marry Drew. And I want to be Natalie's new mommy."

"Then, you have only to believe," Mr. C. whispered. "Natalie already knows that." He winked confidentially as Holly considered that, then leaned forward to gently blow.

A thousand tiny snowflakes took flight from the wrapping paper clutched in Holly's hands. Holly saw now that there was a sprinkling of fairy dust there, the same dust that had sent her spinning from the North Pole workshop to here, the same dust that could make a million dreams come true in a single night.

Just as it would make her dream come true.

Holly laughed as the shimmering light surrounded her, as the flakes swirled and danced. They reflected the light from the Christmas tree as if she was in the middle of a crystal snowstorm. The flakes landed on her lips, her cheeks, her hands, her brow. They melted against her skin and Holly felt a subtle change roll through her body.

Holly understood exactly what that change was. She knew with sudden certainty that the only magic in her life from this point on would be the magic that Drew awakened with his touch.

That suited Holly just fine.

When the last flake of fairy dust shimmered to nothing and Holly Berry turned to thank Mr. C. for his gift, he was gone.

There were those new parcels beneath the tree and the stockings on the hearth were stuffed. The cookies and milk that Natalie had left out had disappeared, but otherwise the room looked just the same as it had before Mr. C.'s visit.

Holly could feel within herself that there had been a real change. In fact, she felt tired in a way she never had before. She sat down in an armchair opposite the tree with a yawn. Holly picked up Drew's gift and closed her fingers around the box as she smiled in anticipation of what the morning would bring.

But her newly mortal body was a little less enthused about staying awake that long. She turned off the lights, remembering her promise to Drew, then settled back in her chair and yawned. She didn't really believe it possible but when the clock struck three, her eyes drifted closed.

For the first time ever, Holly Berry fell asleep, only to find sugarplums dancing in her dreams.

"SANTA WAS HERE!"

A certain six-year-old's cry of delight awakened Holly with a snap. She rubbed her eyes and sat up, blinking when she was confronted by Mr. Bumbles himself, not six inches away from her nose.

Lurking behind the bear was a golden haired cherub wearing jingle-bell earrings, a flannel nightie and big fuzzy slippers. Natalie's eyes were wide.

"Are you going to be my new mommy?" she asked in a stage whisper, as though she didn't dare to hope. "I asked Santa and you're here now."

Holly smiled. "Maybe more like an auntie," she answered, then wrinkled her nose playfully.

Natalie's eyes went round and she threw herself into Holly's arms with unrestrained glee. Holly laughed and hugged the little girl tightly, feeling as though her own heart would burst with happiness.

She glanced up to find Drew leaning in the doorway, his arms folded across his chest and a smile tugging his lips. Holly's heart clenched, then took off at a gallop.

"Unca Drew! Holly's going to be my new mommy!" Natalie raced across the room as her uncle chuckled and scooped her up high.

"So I hear," he murmured. "Merry Christmas, punkin." Drew managed to kiss Natalie's cheek before she squirmed to be set down.

"I have to look in my stocking right now, Unca Drew!"

"Of course." Drew set Natalie down and she dove for the tree.

But Holly had eyes only for Drew. He strolled across the room and retrieved the box that had fallen from Holly's grip while she slept. He opened it as he sat down beside her and removed the delicate ring.

Drew held it an inch away from Holly's hand and arched a brow as he looked into her eyes. "Sure?"

"Absolutely," Holly declared then pushed her finger through the golden circle. Drew grinned and caught her chin in his fingertips, then bent to kiss her.

"Merry Christmas, Holly," he said softly, just before his lips closed over hers. Holly twined her arms around his neck and kissed him back, knowing without a shadow of a doubt that she had made the right choice.

She could tell by Drew's kiss that he thought so, too.

"There's no mistletoe here," Natalie protested long

moments later. Holly and Drew parted reluctantly, then glanced as one to the little girl.

"Sometimes you don't need mistletoe," Drew said solemnly.

"Unca Drew, you just want to kiss my new mommy," she accused with childish conviction.

Drew didn't let Holly go. "Caught me, punkin." He winked at Holly. "That's *exactly* what I want to do."

Holly sighed with contentment and nestled against his warmth. "I suppose we should look under the tree," she teased.

"I've already found the best present," Drew declared and gave Holly a squeeze.

"Me, too!" Natalie declared. The little girl wriggled in between the two of them, Mr. Bumbles in tow. She granted Holly and Drew each a wet kiss, then sat back with a delighted grin to eye the shambles she had left of her stocking. There was still a gleam of anticipation in her very blue eyes.

"Mr. Bumbles says this *is* the bestest Christmas ever," she said with satisfaction. "I told him it would be."

Holly could only agree.

ABOUT THE AUTHOR

Deborah Cooke sold her first book in 1992, a medieval romance published under her pseudonym Claire Delacroix. Since then, she has published over fifty novels in a wide variety of sub-genres, including historical romance, contemporary romance, paranormal romance, fantasy romance, time-travel romance, women's fiction, paranormal young adult and fantasy with romantic elements. She has published under the names Claire Delacroix, Claire Cross and Deborah Cooke. **The Beauty**, part of her successful Bride Quest series of historical romances, was her first title to land on the *New York Times* List of Bestselling Books. Her books routinely appear on other bestseller lists and have won numerous awards.

In 2009, she was the writer-in-residence at the Toronto Public Library, the first time the library has hosted a residency focused on the romance genre. In 2012, she was honored to receive the Romance Writers of America's Mentor of the Year Award.

Currently, she writes paranormal romances and contemporary romances under the name Deborah Cooke. She also writes medieval romances as Claire Delacroix. Deborah lives in Canada with her husband and family, as well as far too many unfinished knitting projects.

Visit her websites to learn more:

http://DeborahCooke.com
http://Delacroix.net

10. When Annika Met Thom

Annika and Thom

Flatiron Five Tattoo

1. Just One Snowbound Night

(Olivia and Spencer)

2. Just One Vacation Night

(Reyna and Kade)

3. Just One Unforgettable Night

(Lexi and Gabe)

4. Just One Christmas Night

(Chynna and Trevor)

The Coxwells

1. Third Time Lucky

(Philippa and Nick)

2. DOUBLE TROUBLE

(James and Maralys)

3. ONE MORE TIME

(Matt and Leslie)

4. ALL OR NOTHING

(Zach and Jen)

5. Christmas with the Coxwells

Novellas

A Berry Merry Christmas

Coming in 2025

a new series of contemporary romances

from Deborah Cooke.

Watch for

Just Trouble

The Carpe Diem Café #1

In February 2025.